TOM SWIFT AND HIS REPELATRON SKYWAY

From the very moment that Tom Swift Jr. agrees to help the government of Ngombia build a highway to link the jungle-separated provinces of the new African nation —a task that has stumped the best engineers in the United States—he is beset by mysterious attacks aimed to defeat the project.

Construction of the road is urgent. At stake is the economic future of this friendly country. But no conventional highway will do. For existing engineering methods can not be used to bridge the seething, bubbling swamp in the rain forest.

Tom comes up with an amazing scientific solution to the problem—an aerial highway over the jungle at tree-top level, supported only by invisible repelatron beams.

Deep in the jungle, fantastic-sized creatures—throwbacks to the dinosaur age—and an eccentric scientist, missing for twenty years, add to the harassments besetting the Swift work crews.

In a series of dangerous adventures, Tom must out-maneuver the sinister forces working against him and the Ngombian government, win the trust of the hostile scientist, and carry through the skyway to a successful conclusion.

*Monsters of nightmarish size plunged through
the camp*

THE NEW TOM SWIFT JR. ADVENTURES

TOM SWIFT
AND HIS REPELATRON
SKYWAY

BY VICTOR APPLETON II

ILLUSTRATED BY EDWARD MORITZ

NEW YORK

GROSSET & DUNLAP PUBLISHERS

CONTENTS

CHAPTER I

THE DEVIL DOLL

"WHAT do you call this automatic skywriter?" asked Bud Barclay.

His friend Tom Swift Jr. was piloting a new helicopter over Lake Carlopa. The strange-looking craft was emitting a stream of red luminous gas.

"Watch," said Tom. "As I trace words with a stylus on this sensor panel, a computer will steer the ship and skywrite the message."

In a moment the ship was turning and maneuvering so that its luminous stream formed the words:

THIS IS THE NEW SWIFT GRAPHICOPTER

"Wow! An advertiser's dream!" Bud exclaimed.

The two eighteen-year-olds were seated in the control cabin atop the twin-rotored craft. Its fuselage was shaped like a huge TV set, with the sky-writing equipment inside.

Suddenly Bud gasped as he saw a plume of smoke rise from the Forest Park Reservation across the lake. "Good night! A forest fire!"

Tom, a rangy youth with a blond crew cut, gunned the graphicopter toward the woods. An updraft of heated air buffeted the ship as it neared the smoking area.

"This is going to be a real blaze!" Bud said.

"And no lookout station around here, either," Tom muttered anxiously.

Tongues of orange flame could be seen through the smoke, leaping from tree to tree. The fire was spreading toward the main park road.

"With those arching branches, the blaze could easily jump across the road!" Tom exclaimed. "Everybody in the park will be trapped!"

The dark-haired copilot shuddered. "Think we could set this copter down on the road?"

"Not enough clearance. We'd wreck our rotors."

Tom headed the ship in a wide, circling sweep over the woods. At a number of spots the boys glimpsed people grouped around picnic tables.

Tom said grimly, "They haven't the faintest notion yet that a fire has started! I'll radio Enterprises to alert the State Police." Swift Enterprises was a huge experimental station which had its own airfield. But Tom and Bud both realized that there was little hope of patrol cars or mounted policemen broadcasting the alarm in time.

"Let's go down as low as possible," Bud suggested.

Tom swooped to treetop level, and Bud leaned out to bellow at one group of picnickers seated at a table. His voice was drowned by the craft's whirring rotors. The people merely laughed and waved back—obviously unaware of their danger.

"Jumpin' jets! I can't get through to them!" Bud exclaimed in despair. "Drop a ladder, Tom, and I'll do a Paul Revere act on foot!"

The young inventor shook his head. "You'd be trapped yourself, fly-boy, before half the people in these woods got the word."

"But we must do *something!*" Bud insisted.

"We're going to," Tom replied calmly. "When you mentioned this graphicopter's being an advertiser's dream, I was about to explain that it has other uses. You'll see one right now!"

Heading the craft on a course straight across the woods, Tom began writing on the sensor panel:

FOREST FIRE! NO CAUSE FOR PANIC
BUT LEAVE PARK IMMEDIATELY!
MAIN ROAD BLOCKED. USE WEST EXIT

As Tom wrote, the ship automatically began painting the words in huge, luminous red letters across the sky. Next, Tom switched the skywriter's color selector and added a sweeping green arrow, pointing out the direction of the proper exit.

"Boy, this is the greatest thing since the invention of the fire engine!" Bud declared. "How long will the writing keep its shape before the paint or gas—or whatever it is—scatters?"

"It won't scatter at all, although the lines of writing may drift with the air currents." Tom added that if the arrow were blown out of line, he might have to blot it out and paint a new one. "But the letters should remain distinct for several hours before they fade."

Tom explained that the colored gas used for the "sky paint" contained ions of Inertite. This was a substance which Tom had extracted from rocks taken from the caves of nuclear fire in Africa. After exposure in the laboratory to radiation, the Inertite began to generate a continuous high-energy field which made the molecules of gas cling together.

Tom's skywritten warning had an immediate electrifying effect on the picnickers. They doused their fires and hurried toward the west exit.

"Here come the fire fighters!" Bud exclaimed. Several fire trucks could be seen speeding toward the reservation.

Meanwhile, Tom flew a careful search pattern over the woods to make sure all campers and picnickers were safely on the way out. Satisfied that no one was in danger, he headed back to the fire.

By this time it was a raging inferno, glowing like a furnace under the billowing clouds of black smoke. Firemen were playing streams of water along the flanks of the blaze. A crew of state troopers and volunteers were frantically trying to chop out a firebreak with bulldozers and axes.

"They'll never make it in time to save the reservation," Bud muttered.

Tom was thinking the same thing. He radioed the State Police command car that the reservation

*Tom's warning had an electrifying effect
on the picnickers*

appeared to be clear of people, then asked if help was needed to fight the fire.

"Definitely!" Captain Rock replied. "A fire in the reservation is so unexpected at this time of year that there are no tanker planes on call."

"Stand by," Tom radioed back. "Maybe I can give you a hand."

Quickly he called Enterprises and ordered that a tank of Tomasite emulsion be rushed out to the airfield. Tomasite was an amazing insulating plastic developed by the young inventor's father, Tom Swift Sr. Tom Jr. had produced a liquid form for use as a fire-extinguishing chemical.

Within minutes, the boys landed at the Swifts' experimental station, a vast four-mile-square enclosure dotted with gleaming modern research laboratories and workshops.

"When I designed this copter," Tom explained to Bud as they climbed out of the ship, "I had in mind a fuselage that could be adapted to a number of different uses, such as crop-dusting, spraying, fire fighting, or aerial transport."

Under Tom's supervision, the skywriting equipment was hastily removed from the hollow fuselage and the tank of Tomasite emulsion installed, with an operating-control linkage. The changeover was completed in less than fifteen minutes.

The two boys took off again for the reservation. Mobile TV cameras, which had arrived to televise the fire-fighting action, tilted skyward for a view of the strange-looking helicopter.

"We're carrying a tankful of extinguisher," Tom radioed Captain Rock. "I'll start my run now."

"Thanks, Tom! Good luck!" came the response.

A wave of heat seared the craft's cabin as Tom guided the graphicopter over the fire. Only his skillful piloting held the craft on course against the buffeting of the thermal updraft.

"Man! It's like looking into an open furnace!" Bud gasped, shielding his eyes from the glare.

Tom was already manipulating the tank's dump valve. Bud moved aft to watch as the Tomasite emulsion spewed downward in the graphicopter's wake.

"It's working like a charm, Tom!" he reported. "Seems to be damping out the flames."

After several passes over one of the burning areas, Tom had completely checked the blaze.

"Sorry my tank's empty," Tom radioed, "otherwise I'd douse the whole fire for you."

"No need. It's under control now," Captain Rock replied. "Tom, the TV boys want you to land for an interview. You're a hero!"

The young inventor chuckled. "You're in charge, Captain—you give 'em an interview. Bud and I were just the visiting firemen."

The boys landed at the Enterprises airfield and Tom sent word to the Senior and Junior Swifts' secretary, Miss Trent, that he would not be available to newsmen. Then he and Bud jeeped to Tom's glass-walled private laboratory.

"Pal, I'd say your new graphicopter is a terrific success," Bud remarked with a grin, settling himself on a lab stool. "Tell me more about it."

"My main reason for inventing the skywriting gear," Tom explained, "was because I felt it would be useful in time of disaster. Messages could be sent to people in a disaster area, where no radio communication is available."

Bud nodded. "The way you alerted those picnickers about the forest fire sure proves that."

"I also have an idea," Tom went on, "that it can be used for laying out luminous flight paths at airports during periods of poor visibility."

"What if there's a breeze?" Bud objected. "You said yourself the skywriting lines may waver or drift. If they went haywire, they might lead an incoming plane right into a bang-up crash."

"True. But, you see, the ionized gas could be held rigidly in line by a magnetic beam projected from the airport."

There was a knock at the door and two pretty girls stepped into the laboratory.

"Hi, Phyl! Hi, Sandy!" Tom exclaimed. Bud echoed his greeting as the boys stood up.

"We came to make sure you two heroes were all right," teased Sandra Swift, Tom's blond seventeen-year-old sister, whom Bud often dated.

"And get, firsthand, your exciting story of the forest fire," added Phyllis Newton. Phyl, a brown-eyed brunette, the same age as Sandy, was the daughter of Ned Newton, Tom Sr.'s old comradein-arms and now manager of the Swift Construction Company.

"We saw your new copter on TV when you two were putting out the fire," Sandy said more seriously. "It was really thrilling!"

"Plenty hot, too," Bud replied with a wry chuckle. "But your modest brother over there is the genius who deserves all the credit."

Tom changed the subject by pointing to a package which Sandy held tucked under her arm. "Don't tell me you've been shopping again, Sis."

Sandy's blue eyes twinkled. "Not this time. It's for you," she added, handing the package to her brother. "It came today in the mail."

Tom took the brown-paper-wrapped parcel and noted the return address on the label. "Um-m, this is from the Ngombian Embassy in Washington, D.C.," he observed in surprise.

"Ngombia? Say, that's in Africa, isn't it?" Bud asked with keen interest.

"Yes," Tom replied. "A new country that gained its independence recently. As a matter of fact," he added, "it's sending an official here to Enterprises tomorrow to discuss some new project. But this package—I have no idea what it contains."

Tom opened the gift as Bud and the two girls watched curiously. Inside was a small, carved African figure with weirdly painted features.

"Ugh!" Phyl gasped. "How scary!"

"That face looks like some kind of devil mask,"

Bud said. "It'd make a great Halloween present."

Tom grinned. "I guess this devil doll is supposed to be a desk ornament. Look! This spear which the figure's holding is a ball-point pen."

To show the others, he pulled out the pen and scribbled a few lines on a sheet of paper.

"Blood-red ink!" Sandy exclaimed. "I wouldn't want that creepy-looking idol on *my* desk!"

"But I'd better put it on mine," said Tom. "The Ngombian representative might be offended if he doesn't see me using the gift."

Sandy and Phyl had to leave soon afterward. Bud offered to escort them to the gate. Tom, who was eager to continue work on one of his experiments, asked his friend to take the devil doll to his office in the main building.

A short time later Bud deposited the strange figure alongside Tom's blotter. On impulse, Bud grinned, plucked out the pen, and began writing a message.

Suddenly he felt dizzy. Bud tried to rub his hand over his eyes, but his muscles refused to respond! He could scarcely lift his arm!

"H-h-help!" Bud gasped hoarsely. Then he swayed and collapsed in the chair!

CHAPTER II

AIRPORT RUSE

TOM, busy testing his sky-paint gas in a magnetic field, heard the lab intercom buzz.

"Please come to your office quickly!" Miss Trent begged. "Something has happened to Bud!"

"Be right there!"

Hurriedly, Tom jeeped to the main building and dashed through the lobby to the big double office he shared with his father.

Bud was slumped in a chair behind Tom's desk, unconscious. Miss Trent and several other employees were leaning weakly against the walls. All of them seemed about to keel over.

"I—I managed to call the doctor," Miss Trent stammered.

Tom acted on a suspicion. Holding a handkerchief over his nose, he darted across the room and flicked on the air-conditioning exhaust fan. Then he called for help over the intercom.

In moments other employees appeared and assisted the victims out to the lounge chairs and settees in the lobby. By this time Doc Simpson, Enterprises' young medic, had arrived. He quickly administered first aid.

Soon Miss Trent was able to relate what had happened. "Bud went into your office to leave that figure on your desk," she told Tom. "A little later I heard him call weakly for help. When I went in to see what was wrong, he had blacked out."

She, too, had felt herself becoming weak immediately after calling Tom and the doctor. Other people who had responded to her cry for assistance had been nearly overcome.

Doc Simpson frowned in puzzlement. "Offhand, this looks like some form of gas poisoning."

Tom hurried back to his office to investigate, trusting that the exhaust fan by now had cleared the atmosphere. His eye was caught by a message written in blood-red ink on his desk pad:

BWANA TOM: WATCH OUT FOR EVIL EYE!

YOU HAVE BEEN VOODOOED BY . . .

The final letters trailed off in a smear.

For a moment Tom was startled. Then he grinned as he recognized Bud's unfinished handiwork. But suddenly a frown came over the young inventor's face. He picked up the devil-doll figure and began to examine it closely.

Tom's perusal was interrupted as Doc Simpson stepped into the office.

"All the victims seem to be okay," the physician reported, "but I'm having them taken to the infirmary just in case."

"What about Bud?" Tom inquired anxiously.

"Still woozy. He seems to have received the worst dose, so I want to give him some further tests and treatments. But judging from his reactions, there won't be any permanent ill effects." Intrigued by the African figure in Tom's hands, Doc Simpson added, "Any clues?"

Tom nodded grimly. "Take a look at this pen socket. There's a tiny capsule in there that must have contained the poison gas!"

Tom explained that he had tried the pen before Bud had. "When I replaced it, evidently the point punctured the capsule. Then, when Bud removed the pen again, the gas came jetting out."

"What a devilish trick!" Doc gasped. "Let me take that over to my lab, skipper. There may be enough traces of the stuff clinging to the capsule to analyze."

As soon as the medic had left, Tom summoned Harlan Ames. The slim, dark-haired chief of Enterprises' security staff arrived shortly. Tom reported the mysterious poison-gas plot.

"Have you checked the Ngombian Embassy?" Ames asked.

"I called it long-distance while you were on the way over," Tom replied. "The ambassador's aide was very upset. He's sure that no such package was sent from their office. But he's going to double-check."

Ames was skeptical that anything would be learned. "Undoubtedly the return address would not belong to the sender. But whoever mailed the devil doll must have known you were expecting a visit from a Ngombian official."

"Right. They're following up on that angle, too," Tom said. "As far as the ambassador's aide knew, no one in this country—except their own embassy members and a few of our people—was aware that they were planning to consult Swift Enterprises."

Ames promised to have the wrappings and the figure itself examined for clues, and to start a full-scale investigation at once. "This deal looks nasty, skipper," he added worriedly before leaving. "From now on, watch yourself!"

Tom agreed to be careful, although he took the situation calmly. The young inventor had become used to coping with dangerous enemies ever since his amazing scientific exploits had first catapulted him into the public eye.

In his first adventure, Tom had fought for his life against a gang of South American rebels aiming to seize a priceless radioactive-ore deposit. Only recently, Tom had struggled to save the Swifts' phantom satellite base from capture by the asteroid pirates.

The following day Ames glumly reported to Tom that neither the devil doll nor the package wrappings had yielded any promising clues.

"Only one thing I can tell you for sure, skipper," Ames said. "That figure is an authentic African carving."

He added that both the United States Postal Inspectors and the FBI were trying to trace the senders.

From the security office, Tom drove to the Enterprises infirmary. He was glad to hear from Doc Simpson that Bud had completely recovered.

"But I'm going to keep him here another day for observation," Doc added. "By the way, I've identified the stuff from that capsule. It's an odorless gas that paralyzes the nervous system."

"Good grief!" Tom shuddered. "How come Bud and the others weren't killed!"

"Sheer luck. The seal around the pen socket wasn't tight, so most of the gas probably leaked off into the open air while Bud was carrying the figure to your office. I imagine there was only a tiny amount to begin with—just enough to kill you the next time you used the pen."

The sender, Doc said, no doubt had hoped that the small amount of gas would dissipate before Tom's body was discovered—thus leaving no clue to the mysterious cause of his death.

"Whew!" Tom was shaken by the news. "We should all be mighty thankful!" he murmured.

In Bud's room Tom found the husky young flier impatient to be discharged from the infirmary.

"You ought to have some influence around here, genius boy," Bud grumbled. "Can't you arrange to get me turned loose?"

"Sorry, pal—not a chance." Tom grinned, and

pulled up a chair beside his friend. The two boys discussed the mystery of the devil doll for a few minutes, then Tom went on, "Seriously, Bud, I'm sorry you can't come with me. I'm going to the airport to meet that Ngombian official."

"Exactly who is he?" Bud asked.

"Name's Kwanu. He's the country's Assistant Minister of Economic Development. I don't know what sort of project they have in mind, but it may be something interesting."

"Keep me posted."

"Right. I think I'll take an atomicar," Tom added, "and give our visitor an aerial view of Shopton and the plant."

Tom Swift's unique atomicars were sleek, atomic-powered vehicles that could operate on land, sea, or in the air.

When Tom arrived at the airport terminal later, a man came rushing up to meet him. "Are you Tom Swift Jr.?" he inquired. As the young inventor nodded, he went on hastily, "We've just had a call up in the airport manager's office from Washington. There's been a change of plans for that African official you were to meet."

Tom's eyebrows lifted inquiringly. "How so?"

"He's being flown here in an Air Force jet, instead of coming by regular airliner," the man explained. "You know—the red-carpet treatment. The jet will land on your Enterprises' airfield, so it's requested that you return there at once to be on hand for his arrival."

Tom frowned. For some reason, the man's story stirred a faint distrust in his mind. Why, Tom wondered, had the message been phoned to the airport instead of to Enterprises?

The young inventor stared keenly at his informer. The man was tall, with thinning dark hair and an oddly wedge-shaped face that tapered from bulging temples down to a sharply pointed chin. It occurred to Tom that he had never seen the fellow at the Shopton Airport before.

"Have you worked here long?" Tom asked.

"Only a few months. Why?"

"Just wondered." Tom added coolly, "If you don't mind, I think I'll go to the airport manager's office myself and make sure I have all the details of the message straight."

The messenger looked surprised, then shrugged. "Just as you like."

Tom thought he detected a faint foreign accent in the man's speech.

The man accompanied Tom as the young inventor started up the stairway to the balcony circling the terminal waiting room. From here, Tom headed down a hallway that led to the personnel offices.

Suddenly, out of the corner of his eye, Tom caught a movement of the man's arm. He was pulling a gun from under his coat! Tom whirled and grabbed for the man's wrist, but his opponent hooked a foot behind Tom's leg and tripped him with a quick push. As the young inventor reeled backward, the gun smashed down on his skull. With a groan of pain Tom blacked out.

Minutes later, he stirred and revived. Tom was in some kind of dark, cramped space. Struggling to his feet, he kicked over what sounded like a metal pail. He groped along the wall, found a doorknob, and twisted it. As the door came open, Tom realized that his assailant had dragged him into a janitor's closet.

"O-oh! My head!" Tom winced as he stepped out into the light.

He glanced along the hallway, then dashed down the stairs to the terminal waiting room. As Tom's eyes roved in search of the man who had knocked him out, he saw a large, distinguished-looking African in a colorful toga. The stranger stood nearby with two attendants.

Tom hurried toward them. "You are perhaps Mr. Kwanu?" he asked.

"That is correct."

"I'm Tom Swift Jr. Forgive me for keeping you waiting."

"Not at all," the African said politely. He introduced his two attendants and added, "We were informed that you had been delayed."

Tom stiffened in surprise. "Informed? By whom?"

"By your assistant from Swift Enterprises. Did you not know?"

"I certainly didn't," Tom said. "Please tell me what happened."

Kwanu explained that he had been met by a man who introduced himself as a representative of the Swifts. He had explained that Tom Jr. would arrive in a few moments to greet the visitors. Meantime, the man would take Kwanu's secretary to the mayor's office in Shopton to arrange the details of an official reception.

"Did your secretary go with him?" Tom asked in alarm.

"Of course."

"What did the man look like?" Tom went on anxiously.

Kwanu seemed puzzled by Tom's questions, but answered, "He was tall, slender, dark-haired. Also, he had a large forehead and a pointed chin."

Tom flushed with anger. "I'm sorry to have to tell you this, but that man is an impostor. He's responsible for the delay in meeting you."

Hastily Tom recounted what had happened to him, and apologized for his disheveled appearance.

"The whole thing was obviously a plot to get me out of the way so that you or your secretary could be kidnapped."

The two attendants were greatly upset by the news, but Kwanu remained calm. Tom notified the airport guards and called the police. An investigation proceeded quickly.

The airport parking-lot attendant recalled seeing a colorfully garbed foreigner, carrying a briefcase, accompanied by two men who appeared to be Americans. One of them answered the description of Tom's assailant. The three had driven off in a dark-blue convertible.

The police sergeant in charge immediately sent out a radio alert to set up roadblocks. Tom volunteered to scout from the air in his atomicar for the kidnapper's automobile. Kwanu and his two attendants insisted upon coming with him.

For half an hour they skimmed and circled over the highways leading from the airport. Suddenly Tom sighted a figure in a striped toga lying near the roadside on a dirt turnoff. He landed and they hurried toward the prostrate form.

"Your secretary is unconscious but still alive," Tom announced, after checking the victim's pulse.

"His briefcase is gone!" Kwanu exclaimed. "It contained full details of the project on which I came to consult you!"

CHAPTER III

A HURTLED WARNING

KWANU'S two attendants searched frantically, but could not find the briefcase. Over the atomicar radio Tom notified the police and summoned an ambulance. When it arrived, an intern examined the secretary.

"He has been chloroformed," the intern said. "Should come out of it soon, though."

Tom and his guests followed the ambulance to the Shopton Hospital. Here Tom himself was examined by a doctor for signs of concussion. Apparently the blow he had received had resulted in nothing more than a swollen bruise.

The young inventor hurried to the room where Kwanu's secretary, Mr. Wumbe, had been taken. By this time he had recovered consciousness. Police Chief Slater and Harlan Ames had arrived to hear his story.

"I left the terminal with the man who claimed to be the Swifts' representative," the secretary related. "Another man was waiting for us near the parking lot. I asumed he was to be our driver, but instead he climbed into the back seat, while I was invited to sit in front."

After driving along a paved highway, Mr. Wumbe went on, the impostor had turned up a dirt road, stopped the car, and pulled a gun.

"He ordered me to hand over the briefcase. Suddenly the man in back grabbed me and held a cloth over my nose. That is all I remember."

"This second man—the one in the back seat—can you describe him?" Chief Slater asked.

Mr. Wumbe thought for a moment. "He is young, muscular looking, and wore a blue suit with an open-necked shirt."

Ames turned to Kwanu. "What about the briefcase? Did it contain any scientific secrets or other valuable information?"

The Ngombian official shrugged. "Valuable to my people and my country, yes. But the information would be worth nothing to an outsider."

"Do you think someone from your country may have been behind the plot?" Chief Slater asked Kwanu.

"Yes, it seems the only answer. You see, we have suffered much political turmoil since we gained our independence, and there are certain factions which would like to block Ngombia's economic progress. I assure you that my embassy will not make a diplomatic incident of what happened today."

Tom exchanged a look of relief with Ames and Slater.

"Thank you for taking that attitude, sir," said the police chief. "We'll make every effort to run down the guilty persons."

As the group was leaving the hospital, Chief Slater was called to the phone. After a few minutes' conversation, he rejoined the others. "The kidnap car has just been found abandoned," he informed them. "It checks with a car that was reported stolen. The kidnappers probably took it to pull this job."

Ames speculated that the criminals could have transferred to another car and thus slipped through the roadblocks unnoticed.

Tom flew the Ngombians and Ames in the atomicar back to Enterprises. Here they gathered around the conference table in the Swifts' office.

"My friend," Kwanu began, facing Tom with a smile, "you and your father have the reputation of doing the impossible. We have, therefore, come to ask you to undertake an impossible task."

Tom grinned back, slightly embarrassed. "Thank you. My father regrets that he can't be here for this meeting—he's engaged on a secret space research job at our rocket base on Fearing Island. I think he'd tell you we can't do the scientifically impossible, but we're certainly interested in hearing about your project."

Kwanu rose and stepped to a huge relief globe of the world which stood near Mr. Swift's desk.

"My country, Ngombia, is divided into two

provinces, inhabited by tribes that differ in customs." Kwanu pointed out their location. "West Ngombia—which is agricultural and settled—contains our capital, Princetown. East Ngombia, more primitive, is rich in minerals which are being mined by an international firm, Afro-Metals, Limited, by arrangement with our government."

"I've heard of it," said Tom.

"Unfortunately," Kwanu went on, "the two provinces are separated by a vast jungle. To weld our country together and develop it, a highway system must be built through this still-unexplored jungle—an almost insurmountable task, according to skilled engineers."

"Has a route ever been surveyed?" put in Ames.

"Yes, quite recently, by an American firm—the Burlow Engineering Company," Kwanu replied. "My government had planned to give them a contract to build the highway. But they encountered an unforeseen problem."

Tom was intrigued. "An unforeseen problem?"

"The jungle is split almost in two by a strange swamp," Kwanu explained. "The highway route must cross this swamp. But Burlow's engineers felt that the bog would not support a roadbed. As a result, their proposal called for a lengthy detour around the swamp and three years' construction time for the highway, at a much higher cost than we expected."

"Then Burlow Engineering is no longer being considered?" Tom asked.

Kwanu shrugged. "I fear they were angry when we rejected their proposal, but we had no choice. Frankly we cannot afford their price, nor can we wait three years for our highway. To make our country stable and prosperous, the two provinces must be linked quickly. We are hoping you can provide the solution."

Tom smiled wryly. "It's a large order."

"The stolen briefcase," Kwanu added, "contained Burlow Engineering's proposal, based on the survey for which we paid. It included complete details on the route, terrain, soil sampling, and other information. Unfortunately, the briefcase also contained the copies of the report which I was bringing for your use. However, the original report is in Princetown, and it will be only a matter of a few days before we can have additional photostats made for you. It would have been a great help to you in assessing the problem if I could have presented the papers to you now."

"It sure would," Tom agreed. "But perhaps I can get a copy from Burlow Engineering faster. I'd like to talk to their people, anyway. This certainly sounds like an interesting and challenging job, but we'll need time to think it over. My father will be back this evening, sir. Could you stay for a further discussion tomorrow?"

Kwanu shook his head. "I fear not. In view of the theft of the briefcase, I must return to Washington at once and make a full report to my government. Then, early tomorrow, I am scheduled to fly to Africa for an important cabinet meeting. In any case, you will no doubt need several days to consider the project before coming to a decision."

"Right, sir," Tom agreed. "And of course we'd want to make a preliminary survey of our own before taking on the job." On this note the meeting broke up.

Mr. Swift arrived from Fearing Island late that afternoon. Upon hearing of the Ngombian project, he telephoned Ned Newton at the Swift Construction Company, which manufactured the inventions developed at Enterprises. That evening Tom and the two older men gathered in Mr. Swift's den to discuss the matter.

"I'd say the project is worth looking into," said Mr. Newton. "We'd be helping a new democratic country in Africa, and a successful job over there would be a credit to America—if you two Toms can lick the engineering problems."

Mr. Swift's eyes lighted with enthusiasm. Trim and boyish looking, with keen blue eyes and only slightly graying hair, he closely resembled his taller, lankier son. "I agree, Ned. However, I'll be tied up on our government aerospace research—which means that Tom here will have to take charge. How about it, son?"

"I'd sure like to try, Dad. With you backing me up on the engineering end, and Uncle Ned on costs, I might be able to handle it."

Tom Sr. smiled at the young inventor. "Any ideas on how to lay this jungle highway?"

"Not exactly," said Tom, "but I'm wondering if a highway is the only answer."

"Meaning what, son?"

"Well, an atomicar transport system might be one solution," Tom explained. "Since the flying cars can operate over any terrain, no regular highway would be needed. That way, we—"

Tom's words were cut short by a spurt of the alarm system. It was followed by the sound of shat-

tering glass as an object streaked through the window and across the room. With a *twang* the missile buried its nose in the opposite wall!

"A spear!" Tom cried.

Leaping from his chair, he dashed over to examine the still-quivering weapon. Attached to its shaft was a piece of paper bearing a crudely printed message in blood-red ink:

TOM SWIFT — STAY OUT OF AFRICA
OR YOU AND YOUR FAMILY WILL SUFFER!

Mr. Swift and Uncle Ned hastened to Tom's side as he read the message aloud. At the same time, Sandy and her slender, pretty mother came hurrying into the den.

"Oh!" Mrs. Swift gasped anxiously.

"Why didn't the warning buzzer keep ringing?" Sandy asked, bewildered.

"It was the spear that touched off the alarm," Tom guessed. "Whoever threw it must have stayed outside the range of the alarm."

The Swift home was surrounded by an electromagnetic field that gave warning of any intruder. Tom and his father had provided the family and their friends with wristwatches containing tiny deactivator coils to avoid setting off the system. Anyone without such a device was detected as soon as he broke the field.

Using a handkerchief to protect any possible fingerprints, Tom worked the spear loose from the wall. Then he and Mr. Newton dashed outside the house. Mr. Swift had already switched on flood-lights and was unkenneling the Swifts' two blood-hounds, Caesar and Brutus.

Tom let the dogs sniff the spear to get the scent. But after loping about the grounds, the hounds gave up in whimpering bafflement.

"The spear must have been hurled from a passing car," Tom decided.

Mr. Swift nodded. "I believe I recall hearing one approach just before the alarm sounded."

"Whoever threw it must have been someone of giant strength," said Mr. Newton in an awed voice as he eyed the distance from the street. "It was buried inches deep in the wall!"

"Or it might have been projected by a powerful, specially designed spear gun," Tom conjectured.

After telephoning Ames and the police, Tom turned to his father. "Dad, you don't think we should give up this project, do you?"

"No," said Mr. Swift. "We'll decide about the project on its own merits, son. I'm opposed on principle to yielding to threats."

Tom gave his father a warm handclasp. "So am I!" he declared.

Next morning, Tom checked with Harlan Ames and was debating whether or not to call Washington when an Enterprises messenger delivered a telegram. The message was from Kwanu. He said officials in Princetown had advised him by transatlantic telephone that *every* copy of the

Burlow report had been stolen from the offices of the Ministry of Economic Development in Princetown!

"That," said Tom, making a quick decision, "settles it!"

Without further delay, Tom flew to Newark to interview Ben Burlow, president of Burlow Engineering Company, about the Ngombian highway survey. The young inventor gave his name to a receptionist in the company's office lobby. A moment later a rugged-looking, gray-haired man burst from one of the offices, his face red with anger.

"So you're Tom Swift, eh?" he growled. "Get out of here before I throw you out!"

CHAPTER IV

VOODOO STEW

TOM was startled by the man's furious outburst, but said calmly, "If you're Mr. Burlow, I've flown all the way from Shopton to see you. Please hear what I have to say."

"I'm Burlow, all right!" the man stormed. "As for hearing you, I'd say you've talked too much in this story!" He waved a newspaper in front of Tom's face.

Tom took the paper and glanced at the article Burlow pointed out. The next moment Tom flushed with annoyance and embarrassment.

The story was headlined: TOM SWIFT WINS "IMPOSSIBLE" JOB IN AFRICAN JUNGLE. It stated that Swift Enterprises had just announced that it was contracting with the Ngombian government to lay a jungle highway which other engineers claimed would take three years to build. The story was full of boastful quotes, attributed to Tom, about how easily Swift Enterprises would handle the project.

Several slurring remarks, supposedly made by Tom, were included about the firm which had lost out on the project.

"So you think you can do a better job than Burlow Engineering!" the company president raged. "Why, you young pup, you aren't even—"

"Look, Mr. Burlow," Tom cut in coldly, "I know nothing about this story. Swift Enterprises has made no such announcement, and I've given out no interview. Those alleged remarks of mine are as much of a shock to me as they were to you."

Burlow stared at the young inventor in disbelief. "In that case, where did the story come from?"

"I don't know, but I intend to find out," Tom replied. "We haven't even agreed to take on the job."

"Very well," the company president said grudgingly. "Come with me."

Tom followed him into Burlow's private office, where he was gruffly invited to sit down. Burlow regarded Tom with a scowl of mistrust.

"All right," he rumbled. "What's on your mind?"

"So far, Swift Enterprises has merely been *asked* to take on the Ngombian highway project," Tom began. "We haven't even looked over the terrain yet. The job must involve terrific problems if a topflight, experienced firm such as yours would need three years to handle it."

Burlow looked somewhat mollified.

"Before going any further," Tom went on,

"we'd like to know what we're up against. That's why I came to see you."

Tom had an added reason for his visit. He was hoping to glean some hint of whether Burlow Engineering might be connected with the sinister events of the past two days.

"You came to the right place, son," Burlow said with relish. "If any outfit can lay that highway in less than three years, I'll eat my hat!"

Tom shrugged. "You may be right. However, I would like to study the proposal you submitted to the Ngombian government."

"Why should I let you see that?" Burlow snapped.

"The engineering details and specifications could save us a lot of time in sizing up the project."

Burlow snorted. "If you think I'm about to help a competitor, you're wrong!"

"The Ngombian government paid for your survey," Tom pointed out. "Surely they should be able to make use of the results."

"Then ask them. They have copies."

"They *did* have," Tom explained, "but every copy has been stolen. The last ones were stolen from the secretary of the Ngombian official who came to see us yesterday."

Burlow stared in amazement, then burst into a loud bray of laughter. "Too bad, Swift. In that case, I guess you're just out of luck!"

Tom stifled the angry retort that rose to his lips. "Then you won't cooperate?"

"That's right. If you geniuses at Swift Enterprises want to take on the job and show us up, go ahead and find out the facts for yourselves."

Burlow's eyes crinkled in a foxy smile as he added, "I'll tell you one thing, though, boy—you have a real unpleasant surprise coming if you think you can lay a highway straight across that jungle swamp. You'll soon find out why we called for the detour that jacked our price up so high!"

Tom realized that it would be useless to press Burlow further. Changing his tack, he questioned the engineer bluntly about the devil doll and the spear incidents, as well as the kidnapping of Kwanu's secretary. Burlow seemed genuinely bewildered—so much so that he even failed to take offense at Tom's implied suspicions.

"Looks as though someone's trying to scare you off the project," Burlow agreed. "But if you suspect us, you're barking up the wrong tree."

"Who else would have any reason to try?"

"Search me," Burlow said with a shrug. "I've heard there are rebellious groups in East Ngombia who don't want the country linked up with a highway—but just rumors, no facts. Better ask the Afro-Metals people. They know more about what goes on in the eastern province than the government does."

"Maybe I'll do that," Tom said, getting up to leave. "Meanwhile, thanks for your time."

Still nettled over Burlow's attitude, Tom flew back to Enterprises. Here he learned that reporters and news services had been phoning his office, asking for more details on the African project. Tom issued a statement denying the original story. Then he hurried to the security office to discuss the matter with Harlan Ames.

"I've just finished checking out that phony article," Ames reported. "Your father heard about it just before he flew back to Fearing Island this morning, and he told me to run it down."

"What did you find out?" Tom asked.

"The story came from a fake news release sent out last night—ostensibly by the Ngombian Embassy in Washington. When I called them, they claimed to know nothing about it. They said they were as surprised as we were."

Tom frowned. "Harlan, this thing really has me baffled. Any leads yet on the devil doll or last night's spear-thrower?"

"Not a thing, skipper," Ames said ruefully. "The paper on which the warning message was printed turned out to be ordinary dime-store scratch paper. And there were no prints on either that or the spear. By the way, the spear itself is an authentic African weapon."

"*Hmm.*" Tom considered thoughtfully. "That seems to point back to Africa again, just like the devil doll. Maybe Kwanu's hunch was right."

Noon found Tom in the Swifts' spacious double office deep in thought over the mystery. He was interrupted by the clumping of cowboy boots in the corridor. Chow Winkler wheeled in a lunch tray.

"Soup's on, boss!" came his foghorn voice.

Chow, a former Texas range cook, was sun-burned and roly-poly. Balding, with a heart as warm as the desert sunshine, he had met the Swifts during one of their trips. Later, he had come East to serve as chef for Tom and his father at Enter-prises and also on their scientific expeditions.

"Hi, Chow!" Looking up, Tom noticed that despite a gaudy lemon-yellow shirt which Chow was sporting that day, the cook seemed troubled. "Anything wrong, old-timer?"

"Jest thinkin' about them queer African goin's-on around here," Chow confided. "First, that ugly lil ole idol what squirted pizen gas, an' then that spear-throwin' last night. Brand my skillet, Tom, I'm plumb worried! What's behind it all?"

"Wish I knew," Tom said. "Maybe it's just someone's idea of a joke—a 'sick' joke, that is. Whoever's responsible, he's bound to trip himself up sooner or later, and then the police or the FBI will take care of him."

"Sure hope you're right." Chow looked relieved as he went on, "Didn't want you sendin' out fer cold sandwiches, boss, so I brought you over some nice mulligan stew today. Jest wait'll you—"

As he lifted the cover from the pot to ladle out the stew, Chow's voice suddenly trailed off in an eerie screech.

"Chow! What's wrong?" Tom asked, jumping up. The cook's face had turned sickly pale.

"Th-there in the pot, boss!" Chow quavered. "T-t-take a look yourself!"

Tom peered into the stewpot and gasped. Inside, in place of the expected steaming mulligan, lay a small clay voodoo figure! It was molded in the shape of a cowboy, with an enormous paunch and ten-gallon hat. The figure was stuck full of pins!

"B-b-brand my grubsack, it's me!" Chow wailed, as Tom pulled out the tiny voodoo doll. "Them p-pins mean I'm marked fer d-d-death!"

The roly-poly cook was trembling like an aspen in a high wind.

"Now, hold it, Chow!" Tom said calmly. "Don't come all unglued. Maybe someone's pulling your leg."

"Pulling his leg?" said a third voice. Bud Barclay walked into the office wearing an innocent smile. "Who would do such a thing to a fearless Texan like Chow?"

The cook stared at Bud, openmouthed for a moment, then exploded into wrath. "Buddy boy! You're the varmint what done it!" he howled. "Shoulda knowed you was up to somethin' when you came sneakin' 'round the galley!"

Bud ducked, half expecting Chow to hurl a plate at him. But the cook quickly recovered his good humor as the boys collapsed with laughter.

"Reckon you got a right to laugh," Chow conceded with a chuckle. "Who'd want to hoodoo a good ole honest Texas trail cook anyhow?"

The two boys were just finishing lunch when Tom received a call from the main gate. A visitor named Darcy Creel, a free-lance zoo collector and journalist, was asking to see Tom.

"If he wants an interview on the African project, no," Tom replied.

"He says that's not why he came," the guard reported. "It's about a special matter that he'd like to discuss with you privately."

Tom hesitated. "All right, send him up."

"Incidentally, he has a camera, skipper. Want it left here at the gatehouse?"

"No, it's okay, provided he takes only authorized photos."

Both Tom and Bud were curious about the unexpected visitor. Darcy Creel turned out to be a blond, young-looking man of about thirty with a slender, wiry build. He was carrying a miniature camera in a case slung around his neck.

"Thanks for seeing me," Creel said as Tom invited him to sit down. "I told the guard I didn't come about your African highway project, but that's not quite true."

"How so?" Tom was instantly cautious.

"Well, I read about this Ngombian business in the paper," Creel explained, "and it happens I've been hoping to go there. But I can't afford an expedition of my own, so I wondered if you might allow me to go with your outfit."

"What's so interesting in Ngombia?" Bud put in.

"I'm marked fer d-d-death!" Chow wailed

"The whole African continent is exciting," Creel replied. "On any trip there I could find material for articles and pick up a few zoological specimens. But Ngombia intrigues me especially."

"Why?" Tom asked.

"I've heard rumors about huge animals of an unknown species existing in the Ngombian rain forest," Creel said. "It's never been properly explored—I might make an outstanding zoological find. And I could be useful to you, too."

Tom considered his visitor. Creel seemed pleasant, and Tom could understand a collector's interest. But he knew nothing about the man's background. "I'm afraid I can't give you an answer right now," Tom replied. "We're not certain yet we'll take on the Ngombian project."

Suddenly a bell rang shrilly.

"It's the plant radar alarm!" Bud cried out.

The boys dashed to the radarscope. Faint blurs of "snow" dotted the screen. Tom snatched up the telephone and called the security office.

"What's happening, Harlan?" he inquired.

"We don't know yet, skipper," Ames replied excitedly. "Some strange metal objects are fluttering down over the plant!"

CHAPTER V

A JUNGLE MYSTERY

TOM hastily excused himself to Creel and ran out of the building, with Bud at his heels. On the way, Tom told Bud what Ames had reported.

"There they are!" Bud exclaimed, pointing upward. A number of small, silvery forms could be seen, glittering in the sunshine as they floated slowly down to earth.

The boys ran to retrieve one piece that landed nearby. Tom examined it closely.

"What the dickens is it?" Bud asked, mystified.

"Seems to be made of aluminum foil. But don't ask me what it's supposed to be."

The foil had been cut and folded in a strange geometric design that looked oddly birdlike. By this time, other employees had come running across the grounds. They scattered to pick up the pieces of foil.

A short time later Ames joined the boys, bringing another batch of the queer foil "birds" which had floated down to the Enterprises airfield. "What do you make of them, skipper?"

"Beats me." Tom studied the pieces with a frown. "It's an old trick for confusing radar, of course, but what's the purpose?"

"Were they dropped from a plane?" Bud put in.

"No, the control tower says none passed over the plant," Ames replied.

"Must have been projected from outside the plant wall—maybe by someone in a car speeding along the highway," Tom speculated.

"But how could thin foil like this stuff be projected so high in the air?" Bud objected.

"Easy," Tom said. "Stack the stuff together in a tight, compact bundle with some kind of fuse release." He added, "Maybe we ought to make sure this stuff really *is* aluminum foil."

The two boys and Ames hurried to Tom's private laboratory. Here the young inventor examined several pieces of the foil, under X rays and with a Swift spectroscope. When he finished, Tom looked at the others, baffled.

"Just plain aluminum foil, that's all."

Ames, equally puzzled, finally left the laboratory. He promised to launch a thorough search for clues outside the plant wall.

Suddenly Bud snapped his fingers. "Hey, you forgot your visitor, Tom!" he exclaimed.

"Oh—oh. I'd better call and apologize." Picking up the telephone, Tom dialed his office. "Let me speak to Darcy Creel, please," he said when Miss Trent answered.

"I'm sorry, but he's gone," she replied. "He waited quite a while after you and Bud went out. Finally he said he had to leave, but he hoped to hear from you about Ngombia." She added, "He left his phone number. Should I try to reach him?"

"Not now," said Tom, and hung up.

Bud, who was scheduled to test-fly the graphi-copter, went off to the hangar. Tom remained in the lab, puzzling over the aluminum "birds."

He noticed that they were cut in several different patterns. Did their shape have any significance? he wondered. Could they represent some kind of religious symbols or totems that might mean something to a native African?

"Seems pretty farfetched," Tom concluded.

Giving up on the mystery, Tom hopped into a jeep and sped back to Enterprises' main building. He had decided to plunge ahead on the African project as quickly as possible.

First, an on-the-spot survey of the jungle terrain would be needed. Tom had dictated some brief plans for the trip to Miss Trent that morning after his return from Newark.

"I'd better look them over again and make sure I haven't forgotten anything," he said to himself.

When he reached his office, Tom went to his current-project file, which was still unlocked, to take out the folder on Ngombia. To his surprise, it was not there. Tom buzzed Miss Trent on the intercom. "Do you have the Ngombia file?" he asked.

"No, I put it back after transcribing your notes," she replied.

"Doesn't seem to be here."

Miss Trent came into the office. "I'm sure I replaced it," she murmured as she leafed through the file drawer. "Oh, here it is—filed under the M's."

Her face was puzzled as she handed the folder to Tom. "That's strange," she remarked. "I'm sure I put it back in the right place."

Tom's blue eyes flashed with sudden interest. "Are you positive?"

"Well—almost positive." Miss Trent frowned. "You see, it comes right after your father's lab folder on neutron emission. And I remember putting it right behind that."

"Okay, thanks." As Miss Trent went out, Tom sat down at his desk. His mind was racing.

Could Creel have tampered with the file on Ngombia when he was left alone in the office?

Tom hastily checked the folder. Everything seemed to be there—the correspondence with the Ngombian Embassy; a transcript of the conference with Kwanu; Tom's plans for his survey trip.

Darcy Creel could have read them all, Tom realized—even photographed them with his miniature camera. The shower of aluminum foil might have been a trick to lure Tom away from his office and thus give Creel the opportunity!

Tom phoned Ames and explained his suspicions.

"That may be the answer," the security chief agreed. "Is Miss Trent certain the folder had been moved?"

"No, not absolutely," Tom said. "But if it *was* moved, it sure explains a lot."

"*Hmm.* On the other hand, skipper, if Creel is working for your enemies, what did they hope to find out? You only discussed the project with Kwanu the day before yesterday—they wouldn't expect you to have a complete set of construction plans drawn up."

"Who knows? They can't tell how far we've gone with this thing," Tom said. "For all we know, they might think that Kwanu came here to sign a definite contract with us—in fact, maybe *that's* what they hoped to find out. The fake news story could have been a move to force our hand— and also provide Creel an excuse for coming here."

"You could be right," Ames said. "I'll start checking on the guy now, skipper."

"By the way," Tom added, "have a couple of those aluminum 'birds' sent to the Ngombian Embassy on the next flight to Washington. I'd like to make sure the 'birds' have no African religious significance."

Next morning Ames reported that his investigation had drawn a complete blank. "Creel seems to be just what he claims. He's well known as a magazine writer and lecturer, and several zoos have bought animals from him."

Tom frowned in bewilderment. "Well, perhaps I'm wrong. But I still can't figure any other reason for that aluminum 'bird' business."

Back at his office, Tom called the Ngombian Embassy. He informed them he planned to fly to Africa the next day for a preliminary survey of the highway route. He also learned that the aluminum "birds" had been checked by their cultural attaché and were not African totem symbols. The rest of the morning Tom spent in rounding up supplies for the expedition, organizing a crew, and laying out flight plans.

After lunch the young inventor drove to the Shopton Museum to see his elderly friend Dr. Gorde, the curator. Tom showed him the spear.

"It's definitely of West African workmanship," Dr. Gorde announced, after carefully studying the weapon.

"From Ngombia?"

The curator shrugged. "I can't be that precise, Tom, but it may well be from the area of the rain forest."

Tom next asked about Darcy Creel. It turned out that Dr. Gorde was acquainted with Creel and knew of nothing against him.

"He might be very helpful to you, Tom, with his knowledge of the African bush. He's also acquainted with several native dialects." The curator paused thoughtfully. "By the way, there's a mystery you might help to solve while you're over there."

"A mystery?"

Dr. Gorde nodded. "It involves a man named Professor Welkin Eldreth, a rather eccentric zoologist. He had some theories about a mysterious plant or mineral extract which could change the growth process of living organisms. He went off to Ngombia twenty years ago to pursue his research work and hasn't been heard from since."

"That sounds interesting," Tom said.

"Yes, I'm curious to know what happened to him—and whether or not he had any success with his theories."

"I'll keep my eyes open," Tom promised, "and see if I can pick up any clues."

Tom returned to Enterprises and phoned Darcy Creel. When he told him to be ready for takeoff the next morning, Creel seemed delighted. Tom felt that if Creel was not involved in the mystery, he would be of considerable help. If he *was* in league with the young inventor's enemies, this would give Tom a chance to watch him and perhaps discover who was behind the plot.

Early the next morning the giant silver *Sky Queen* soared aloft from its special runway on the Enterprises airfield. This atomic-powered craft, equipped with jet lifters, had been Tom's first major invention. It was fitted out with the latest research equipment in all fields of science and was often called the Flying Lab.

Tom was at the controls as the ship streaked southeastward across the Atlantic. Bud, having been up all night supervising the tune-up, was asleep in a bunk. Serving as copilot was Hank Sterling, the blond, square-jawed chief engineer of Enterprises. Chow Winkler had come forward to join them in the flight compartment.

All three stiffened in shock as a bloodcurdling scream suddenly sounded over the intercom.

"He-e-elp!" cried a terrified voice. *"Get this monster away from me!"*

CHAPTER VI

IVORY IDOL

"IT'S Bud!" Tom exclaimed. He unhooked his safety belt and sprang from the pilot's seat. "Take over, Hank, while I go see what's wrong!"

Tom dashed aft through the passageway, with Chow waddling excitedly at his heels. When they reached the crew's bunkroom, the two stopped short in astonishment. Bud was flattened on a wall bunk, staring up at one of the weirdest creatures the boys or Chow had ever seen!

The tiny beast was perched on the pillow just above Bud's head. It was leaning forward with its long bony fingers on Bud's temples while it peered down hypnotically into the boy's eyes.

"Great hoppin' horned toads!" Chow gasped. "What kind o' critter is *that?*"

The animal, small enough to nestle in a man's hand, had brownish fur and a long tail. As Chow spoke, it looked up at the two newcomers.

"Good grief!" Tom murmured. "Head lamps for eyes!"

Its huge orange eyes, with pinpoint pupils, seemed to take up most of the creature's face. Large, batlike ears made it look even queerer.

"Don't just stand there!" Bud begged his two friends. "Do something!"

Footsteps came hurrying down the passageway from the lounge, and Darcy Creel poked his head into the bunkroom.

"Oh—oh! I was afraid of that!" he said apologetically. "Come here, Bushy, you little rascal!"

The tiny creature leaped onto Creel's shoulder and disappeared inside his sport jacket.

"You mean that weird goon belongs to you?" Bud growled, sitting up and glaring at Creel.

"Well—er—yes. Little pet I picked up in Kenya last year."

"What is it?" Tom put in with a grin.

"A bush baby—or galago. She's very friendly."

"*Friendly?*" Bud swung down from the bunk, landing on the deck with a furious thump. "When I woke up and saw that spook staring at me upside down I almost did a jet takeoff!"

Chow howled with laughter.

"What's so funny?" Bud demanded.

"You were! A great big buckaroo like you scared out o' his wits by that little critter!"

"I was afraid to move," Bud fumed. "It might have poked my eye out or bit my nose off."

"I take it the thing *won't* bite?" Tom asked.

"No, of course not," Creel said hastily. "I should have asked permission to bring Bushy on board, but I didn't think she'd bother anyone. She was curled up asleep in some of my gear. I didn't think she'd go off exploring."

"Okay, but keep her away from me!" Bud said. Still grumbling, he pulled on his loafers and accompanied Tom and Chow to the flight compartment.

With the *Sky Queen* cruising smoothly at an air speed of well over three thousand knots, the trip to Africa was completed in less than two hours. It was not yet eleven o'clock in the morning when the giant plane swooped down and landed at the airport of Princetown, capital of Ngombia.

A police officer in a white uniform dashed out to greet Tom and his companions. After saluting smartly, he asked the Americans to wait at the airfield until officials from the Economic Ministry arrived to receive them.

"They have been notified by telephone of your landing and are on their way here," he added.

Twenty minutes later two cars stopped outside the Customs Building. Kwanu and some other officials stepped out.

"Welcome to Ngombia, Tom Swift!" Kwanu shook hands with the young inventor in African fashion, slapping palms together lightly. "I trust none of your men were kidnapped while you were awaiting us?" he added with a chuckle.

Tom flushed. "No, indeed, sir. And I apologize once again for the mistreatment your secretary suffered in my country."

"Please, say no more!" Kwanu raised his hand. "I should not have mentioned the matter. Our own security police have been investigating, but as yet have uncovered no clues."

After introductions, the Americans were driven into Princetown. Tom and his party looked around with interest at the small but bustling African metropolis. Squalid huts and rickety old colonial buildings were giving way to houses and apartments of pink, yellow, and white concrete.

In the center of town, modernistic, glass-tiered office buildings were being erected. Kwanu proudly pointed out the imposing law courts and gleaming new University of Ngombia.

"Your country is certainly developing fast," Tom commented admiringly.

"The pace will be even faster when our two provinces are linked by highway," Kwanu said. "Then the whole country will share in the mineral wealth of East Ngombia."

During luncheon at the Ministry they discussed Tom's plans for the highway project.

"I intend to make a survey flight over the whole jungle," Tom said. "But first I'd like to make a trip into the bush to see the terrain."

Kwanu nodded. "I shall have a guide and porters ready for you by tomorrow morning at Imbolu," he promised. "That village is on the outskirts of the rain forest."

Later the Americans said good-by to their hosts

and split up for a tour of the city. Tom and Bud strolled through the native market.

The scene throbbed with color and excitement in the glaring African sunlight. Men, dark-skinned and stalwart, milled about in flowing, brilliantly patterned togas with one shoulder bare. The women were clad in saronglike garments of printed calico, their heads swathed in gaudy kerchiefs. Some carried naked infants, slung papoose style, on their backs. Others balanced trays of food or merchandise atop their heads.

"I guess those trays must be the Ngombian version of supermarket shopping carts," Bud joked.

Some merchants displayed their wares in wooden booths; others had their goods laid out on the ground on raffia mats or banana leaves. Hunks of raw meat, kola nuts, rice, yams, corn, and a variety of fruits and vegetables were offered for the customer's inspection. Constant bargaining went on in a bedlam of high-spirited chatter.

Presently the boys stopped in front of a wood-carver's stall to select some souvenirs. A moment later Tom gasped and clutched Bud's arm.

"Look!" he hissed, pointing to an ivory figure on a shelf at the back of the stall.

Bud's eyes widened. "Wow! Except for the fact that's ivory, it's just like the devil doll with the poison-gas capsule!"

Tom felt a surge of excitement. Perhaps the figure would provide a clue to his unknown en-

emy! He noticed that the carver had stopped work
and was watching them closely.

Indicating the small ivory statue, Tom asked,
"How much?"

"*Nkò mo nto wi.*" The carver shrugged and went back to work.

"Maybe he doesn't speak English," Bud murmured.

"I'll bet he does!" Tom took out his wallet. "We want to buy it. Please name a price."

"*Kise tita!*" The carver shook his head.

As Tom persisted, the native grew excited. A crowd began to gather, muttering ominously.

"Anything wrong? Perhaps I can help."

Hearing a familiar American voice, the boys turned in relief and saw Darcy Creel shouldering his way toward the booth.

"I'd like to buy that ivory figure," Tom explained, "but this man doesn't seem to want to sell it."

Creel glanced at the statue. His face immediately took on a worried look. He spoke a few hasty words to the carver in some African tongue, then turned back to the boys.

"The figure's not for sale," he told Tom. "It represents a native god—Uoshu, or Satan. The statue is sacred."

"But we've seen one just like it back in America!" Bud blurted out.

Creel shrugged. "Uoshu is always represented the same way—with that queer headdress, medicine gourds, and necklace of cowrie shells. Collectors sometimes obtain a sacred idol, but usually the natives are afraid to sell them, for fear of provoking the god's anger."

Tom yielded good-naturedly. "Okay. Thanks for helping us out of a spot."

The boys bought several other items. The

carver thanked them with bows and smiles, and the crowd broke up.

Tom was still somewhat suspicious of Creel because of the possible tampering with the Swifts' files during the aluminum "bird" incident. He decided to check up on Creel's explanation. Before the boys returned to the *Sky Queen,* he telephoned Kwanu and described the ivory figure.

"Your friend Creel is quite correct," Kwanu replied. "Identical figures of Uoshu can be found all over this part of Africa."

"I guess our so-called clue has fizzled out," Tom reported to Bud after hanging up.

Next morning the *Sky Queen* took off for Imbolu. The straggling village was located on the bank of a muddy river which wound eastward into the bush.

As the Americans climbed down from their plane, they were greeted by a tall native. He wore tattered khaki shorts, a stained T-shirt, and a flower-printed pillbox cap.

"Name is Akomo," he told Tom. "I am your guide. Porters and boats are ready."

"Good!" Tom slapped palms with the guide, and introduced himself and the others. "We'll be ready to leave as soon as the boats are loaded."

The party would paddle upriver into the jungle for some miles, then continue on foot. Tom's crewmen removed the necessary supplies from the plane, as chattering villagers pitched in to help the porters carry them to the riverbank and load them aboard two long pirogues.

"Biggest dugout canoes I've ever seen," Bud remarked.

Meanwhile, the attention of the Americans was caught by a herd of lyre-horned Ankole cattle grazing on the grassy slopes.

"Right smart-lookin' beeves," Chow commented.

As Tom and his companions were admiring them, one of the bulls raised his head, glared at the strangers, and pawed the ground. Before the Americans realized their danger, the bull gave a sudden bellow and charged full tilt at the group!

CHAPTER VII

CRAZY LAUGHTER

TOM and his friends scattered as the maddened beast bore down on them. But Chow, who had wandered away from the others, reacted in lightning cowboy style. His hand streaked down to a coil of rope dangling from his belt. In a twinkling, he had made a loop and sent it snaking out over the bull's head!

As the lasso dropped neatly over its target, Chow took a couple of quick turns around the trunk of a nearby kola tree. The rope yanked taut, bringing the bull up short and throwing him heavily to the ground.

Snorting furiously, the animal began heaving himself upright again. But Chow dashed forward and grabbed his huge horns. Twisting the animal's neck, he bulldogged him to the ground.

"Wo! Wo! Kai! Kai!"

Shouting and cheering, the native herdsmen came running to join Chow and take charge of the subdued animal. In moments the roly-poly cook was the center of an admiring throng of villagers.

"*Ako-mālu jagunjagun nla!*" they chanted.

"'*Great bull warrior*,' they're calling you," Darcy Creel translated with a chuckle.

Tom and the others wrung Chow's hand warmly. "Nice work, old-timer!" Tom told him.

"Shucks, it's jest a knack," Chow said modestly. "When you've branded as many bulls as I have, there's nothin' to it."

One plump village woman squeezed Chow's arm. "*Oni áya!*" she murmured admiringly.

"She says you are brave man," put in Akomo. Smiling, he added, "She has no husband. I think she would like to marry you."

Chow blushed, then turned pale with fright.

"They'd make a swell pair," Bud whispered loudly. "Just about the same size and weight."

"Now you hush up, Buddy boy!" Chow roared, as the other Americans exploded with laughter.

Soon the supplies and equipment were safely stowed aboard the pirogues. Tom exchanged a final handshake with Hank Sterling, who, with two crewmen, would remain to guard the *Sky Queen*.

"Take care, skipper," Hank warned.

"Right. You do the same," Tom replied. "We should be back in a few days. Meantime, keep the ship's radio tuned for reports."

A few minutes later they took their places in the dugout canoes—Tom and Bud in the lead boat with Akomo; Chow and Creel in the other. With shouted farewells, the villagers helped the men shove off into midstream.

Paddles dipped and flashed as the pirogues shot forward through the muddy green water. Clumps of oil palms, mangroves, and bamboo fringed the banks. The oarsmen, muscles rippling in the hot sunshine, soon glistened with perspiration.

Presently the river wound its way into denser vegetation and Imbolu was lost to view. Ahead loomed the Ngombian rain forest—green, somber, and mysterious.

"Makes you wonder what's waiting for us in there," Bud murmured.

Both boys started as an enormous crocodile scuttled into the water from a nearby sand bar.

"Whew! I didn't even see him till he moved!" Bud gulped.

As the canoes penetrated into the forest, the trees became larger and taller, thrusting two hundred feet and more into the air. The arching canopy shrouded the jungle in greenish gloom.

Many of the trees were buttressed with roots spreading outward, high above the ground. Flowering lianas and vines hung in loops and festoons from the branches. Below was a dense tangle of head-high vegetation, much of it with leaves of reddish and purplish hues.

"Those plants never get direct sunshine," Creel explained, "so the red-purple colors enable them to benefit from the sunlight that isn't absorbed by the green leaves higher up."

Chow grunted. "I may turn reddish purple myself 'fore I get out o' this here jungle steam bath!" he muttered, mopping his brow.

Reeds and water weed gradually slowed the strokes of the paddlers. At last the river made a sharp bend, becoming little more than a swampy marsh. Here the canoes were unloaded.

After a brief lunch the porters shouldered their loads, and the party struck eastward into the forest. The trail hacked out by Burlow's survey teams was still visible, though the jungle growth was rapidly obliterating it.

Tom studied the terrain with growing respect. "Now we know what those guys were up against."

A short distance later the trekkers found their way blocked by a rampaging column of black driver ants which swarmed across the trail.

"Nothing turns them aside but fire," Akomo explained to Tom. "Sometimes not even fire. It is better we wait."

Squatting, Chow removed his Stetson hat and fanned his dripping face. "Plumb disgustin' I call it," he snorted, "when a self-respectin' cowhand has to wait fer a herd o' trail-drivin' ants!"

"Ever been stung by one?" Creel put in.

"If I ain't, I reckon it's the only critter what *hasn't* sampled me. What's it feel like?"

"Like a red-hot needle—that won't come out," Creel replied. "You can yank off the body and head, but the ant's jaws stay locked on. The natives once used them for stitching up wounds."

"Even elephants fear these ants," Akomo added. "I have seen them strip a leopard to his bones."

Chow gulped. "Mebbe it won't hurt to sit a spell, at that," he said.

More than two hours were lost before the march resumed. At last the equatorial twilight closed in and Akomo called a halt. Soon the tents had been pitched and campfires were blazing as the jungle cries and twitterings gave way to the steady drone of crickets.

"These jungle animals sure are sneaky," Bud quipped. "I haven't got a good look at one yet, except for a few monkeys."

Just then something fell out of a tree and hit him on the head.

"Ouch!"

Creel pounced on the object. It looked like an oversized pine cone as he held it up to the firelight. "You spoke too soon, Bud," he said.

"What in tarnation is that?" Chow asked.

"A long-tailed pangolin—a real prize!"

The anteater was curled in a tight ball, with its head completely hidden under the tail. It was covered with horny, overlapping scales.

"There must be something about your head that attracts queer animals," Tom teased his pal.

"Guess I'd better get a new one!" Bud grinned.

The evening meal had been eaten before the pangolin consented to uncurl itself. The little creature had a pointed snout, a long tail, and a scaleless white underbody. After some coaxing by Creel, it began to lap up a mixture of chopped meat and raw egg with its wormlike tongue that flicked in and out at lightning speed.

"Our first zoo specimen!" Creel gloated.

"It's all yours!" Bud grumbled.

That night Tom awoke with a start, his ears ringing with a fearsome noise. The stillness was shattered again by a series of terrifying howls and barks—ending in a shrill peal of insane laughter.

"Good grief! Then I wasn't just dreaming!"

Bud joined him as he pulled aside the insect netting and stepped out of their tent. Another peal of crazy laughter sent chills coursing down their spines.

"What in the world is it?" Bud murmured in awe.

"Nothing to fear—only hyenas," Akomo said. He stirred the campfire. As it blazed up, the boys saw the creatures' eyes glinting from the bush.

Chow, who had just poked his head out of his tent, chuckled in relief. "Brand my nightshirt, I thought it was Buddy boy pullin' another joke!"

Late the next morning, as the party was trekking onward, Creel drew his companions' attention with an excited cry. They looked just in time to see a turkeylike bird scuttle off among the underbrush. Its head, Tom had noticed, was crowned with a tuft of white feathers.

"A Congo peacock!" Creel exclaimed.

"*Mbulu,* it is called," Akomo added.

Creel whirled to face him. "You've seen it before?"

Akomo shrugged. "Three, four times maybe."

"So what?" Bud asked Creel.

"Why, that bird wasn't even discovered till recently, and it's never been recorded outside the Congo! If *that* exists here in the Ngombian jungle, think of the other finds that may be waiting for us!" Turning to Tom, he pleaded, "Give me time to go after it! At least long enough to try for some photos!"

Tom felt a sudden twinge of suspicion. Was Creel using the peacock as a ruse to slip away for some underhanded purpose connected with the plot?

Before the young inventor could repy, Bud spoke up, "Swell! I'll go with you!"

From the look Bud flashed him, Tom guessed that the same suspicion had occurred to his pal.

"Okay. I guess the bearers can use a rest. But don't be gone too long."

On Tom's suggestion, Akomo told two of his men to accompany Bud and Creel. As they disappeared into the underbrush, the rest of the party deposited their loads and prepared to wait.

Soon it was time for lunch. Tom was silent and thoughtful as he ate the tasty meal Chow had prepared from their rations. Hour after hour dragged by with still no sign of the bird hunters. Tom became worried as the afternoon wore on. *Had he made a mistake in letting Creel leave the group? And what about Bud's safety if Creel were indeed in league with Tom's enemies? Once they were off in the bush, away from the main party, almost any kind of "accident" might happen!*

At last Tom could stand the suspense no longer. "Chow, I'm going to look for them!"

"Not without me, boss!"

Taking Akomo with them, the two Americans plunged anxiously into the bush. Both Chow and the guide were able to "cut sign" easily on the missing men. Ten minutes after leaving camp, Akomo suddenly stiffened like an animal at bay.

The guide's reaction was noticed at once by Tom and Chow. As they followed his gaze, their scalps bristled. A group of giant natives had suddenly emerged from among the trees—spears poised menacingly at the three trackers!

CHAPTER VIII

A DUEL OF MAGIC

CHOW'S eyes bulged at sight of the spearmen. Tom could almost hear his own heart beating in the deathly stillness that followed.

The tribesmen looked about seven feet tall. Clad only in loincloths, they carried crude iron swords in sheaths slung from their left shoulders. Arms and necks were looped with glass beads, and their faces were scarred with tribal tattoos. Silently they began closing in.

"Make no move!" Akomo whispered nervously.

"Who are they?" Tom asked.

"Wanguru tribesmen—they live in the forest."

By now the natives were almost within spear-thrust of Tom and his two companions.

"*Oku!*" Akomo greeted them.

The Wangurus made no response, their faces grimly impassive. Tom noticed that most of them were staring at him. At last one of the tribesmen spoke—in a commanding voice: "*Wa!*"

"He say to come with them," Akomo translated.

"Where?" Tom said.

Akomo repeated Tom's question in the native's dialect. The tribesman replied curtly.

"They wish us to come to their village," Akomo explained. "It would be best if we go."

"We're in no position to argue," Tom agreed.

The spearmen led the trio off through the underbrush. After a while they emerged onto a beaten trail. A few minutes later the Wanguru village came into view—a cluster of thatch-roofed huts in a small clearing. A tom-tom began to sound, growing louder as they approached.

"The drummer is spreading news of us through the forest," Akomo whispered.

"Jungle telegraph," Tom muttered to Chow.

Men, women, and children swarmed out to watch as they entered the village. Suddenly Chow gulped and pointed to one of the huts.

A human skull was mounted over the doorway! Other huts displayed the same grisly trophies.

"B-brand my soup kettle!" Chow quavered. "These hombres must be head-huntin' cannibals!"

Tom thought this unlikely in modern Africa, but the sight was disturbing. He wondered anxiously about Bud, Creel, and the two porters. Had they too been captured by the Wangurus?

The procession halted in the center of the village. The spearmen stood at attention.

A man emerged from one of the huts. He was clad in a wrap-around garment of greasy calico, and his face was cold and forbidding. His chin bore a tuft of grayish whiskers, and a small leather pouch dangled at his neck. The spearmen drew aside as he walked toward their three captives.

"The tribal witch doctor," Akomo whispered. "The pouch contains his *grigris*—magic charms."

The witch doctor stopped in front of Tom, his eyes glittering with menace. The young inventor returned his gaze. Realizing that the man was trying to unnerve him, Tom took the initiative.

"Ask him why we were brought here, Akomo."

The witch doctor, who evidently knew some English, broke in sneeringly, "You juju man, eh?" he asked Tom.

"Juju man? What's that?"

"He means you do magic," Akomo explained. "I think he heard you come to build highway."

Tom was startled. "How could he know that?"

"Before you come, drums were telling the news —all the way to East Ngombia. They told how other white men tried to make big trail through jungle and could not. But now the *Oba*—the ruler in Princetown—he send for young white man who make strong juju. He build great machines that fly, and go under water, and he will make big trail."

Tom grinned. "They can call it juju here, if they like. In America we call it science."

The young inventor's smile seemed to enrage the witch doctor. "White man's juju no good in forest!" he ranted. "Uoshu and Sho-sho-go make jungle taboo!"

The name of Uoshu—the devil god—caught Tom's attention. Sho-sho-go, he guessed, must be another African deity.

Meanwhile, the witch doctor continued to rave, in snatches of English mixed with his native dialect. Akomo explained uneasily that he was warn-

ing Tom not to try building a road through the jungle—or else the witch doctor would cast a terrible spell against them.

"If we do build a road, it will be for you and your people," Tom stated. The young inventor tried to explain that the Wangurus would then be able to trade with other tribes and receive more food as well as goods. But this only provoked a fresh outburst from the witch doctor.

"Ornery ole windbag," Chow muttered.

Tom had a hunch that the tribal wizard's attitude was partly caused by spite. More than likely he was jealous of the "young white juju man" and might later on stir up the giant tribesmen against Tom's construction crews.

Suddenly Tom had an idea. "All right," he told the witch doctor. "We'll see who has the strongest juju. Call up your strongest spirits against me. Then I will show you *my* power."

Akomo gasped in dismay. Even the witch doctor seemed taken aback by Tom's brash challenge. Then he bared his yellowish-white teeth in a frightening grin.

"*Kai!*" the witch doctor exclaimed. "Now white man see power of jungle spirit!"

He strode back into his hut. An uneasy silence fell over the village. Presently the witch doctor emerged again. He was wearing a hood of woven sisal fiber, painted with grotesque designs, that completely covered his head and shoulders. The hood was topped with a tall headdress of monkey fur. In one hand he held a gourd; in the other, a carved, double-headed ax.

A murmur of fear and awe arose from the tribesmen. Signaling the drummer for a tom-tom beat, the witch doctor began to dance.

Akomo was trembling. "He hides his face to become an evil spirit," the guide explained. "The medicine gourd is Uoshu's, and the ax is the sign of Sho-sho-go, the thunder god."

As the witch doctor danced, he began to chant and wail. His voice rose to a hideous shriek as he hopped about.

"That caterwaulin' alone could scare the wits out o' any critter," Chow remarked.

Finally the incantation ended. The tribesmen seemed astonished that the two white men still appeared unharmed and unshaken.

After retiring to his hut again, the village wizard reappeared, minus his hood and other paraphernalia. "Uoshu and Sho-sho-go speak to me." He held up five fingers. "They say you have this many days to live. Then you must go 'way from forest— or you and all your men will die!"

Turning to the villagers, the witch doctor repeated his prophecy in the native tongue.

"Okay. Now it's my turn," Tom said. He added to Akomo, "Tell them I'm going to conjure up some powerful drums out of the air—drums that no one can see. The drums will make music to celebrate our coming, because our work will bring good things to all the people of Ngombia."

"What in tarnation you aimin' to do, boss?" Chow asked.

"Watch and see." Tom took out an object that looked like a silver pocket pencil but was actually a small, powerful two-way radio. "Keep your fingers crossed," he muttered, "and let's hope we can get enough volume at this range."

Flicking on the set, Tom held the head of the "pencil" close to his mouth. "Tom calling *Queen*. . . . Come in, please."

Soon Hank Sterling answered. "Queen *to Tom. . . . What's up, skipper?*"

"Can't explain now, Hank. Get that tape recording I made of the big intertribal dance at Leopoldville when we came to find the caves of nuclear fire. Hook it up all ready to play."

"*Roger.*" Then, a few moments later, Hank said, "*All set, skipper.*"

Tom responded loudly, "Drums play!" and hastily tuned the receiver to full volume.

Instantly a surge of powerful, throbbing music swelled through the jungle clearing. The tribesmen fell back—eyes popping. They stared at Tom, then all about the village and upward at the treetops, as if expecting the invisible drummers to materialize out of nowhere.

As the drums continued, accompanied by the sound of native flutes and gourd rattles, the Wangurus were caught up in the irresistible rhythm. They began dancing around, chanting, waving their spears, and stomping. Soon a circle of prancing natives formed around Tom, Chow, and Akomo. When the music ended, they hailed the young inventor with shouts and cheers.

"They say *you* are most powerful juju man in all the forest!" Akomo reported proudly.

"Brand my musical pots and pans, you showed that medicine man a thing or two!" Chow added.

The witch doctor had shrunk back, his face contorted with jealousy. Tom decided that now was a chance to win him over. After explaining to Hank, Tom went over to the wizard and offered to teach him how to use the "grigri."

"It is a radio," he said. "A kind of charm."

At first the witch doctor looked as if he could hardly believe Tom would lend him such a powerful charm. He listened eagerly as the young inventor showed him how to work the set and said he had once seen a big radio. Holding the "pencil," he stepped forward and shouted that he, too, would call up the invisible drums.

"Drums, play!" he spoke into the tiny microphone, then turned up the receiver control the way Tom had shown him. Once again the powerful music throbbed through the village, and the tribesmen repeated their wild dance.

Afterward, the witch doctor embraced Tom. "I, Nkoru!" he said, pointing to himself.

"And I'm Tom Swift," the young inventor responded with a smile.

"We brothers!" Nkoru announced. "Now I call on Uoshu and Sho-sho-go ask them not to hurt you."

The witch doctor donned his ceremonial garb again and made another incantation. By the time he had finished, Tom realized it would soon be sunset. The young inventor hoped that he and Chow and Akomo would be allowed to return to their camp. Instead, Nkoru informed them that a feast would be held in their honor.

Huge campfires were lighted, then the women busied themselves preparing the meal. This consisted of a tasty stew of meat, rice, and pimentos cooked in palm oil and served in heaping bowls. The main course was topped off with sweet-tasting balls of yam and cassava paste.

Chow groaned and loosened his belt. "Brand my bakin' sody, I ain't ever et so much!"

"Thank goodness the Wangurus don't seem to be head-hunters after all," Tom remarked with a grin.

Nkoru explained that the skulls belonged to dead members of the tribe. Months after burial, their bones were dug up and the witch doctor examined the skulls for certain signs indicating good luck or bad luck. If the auguries were good, the skulls were kept and displayed as charms against evil spirits.

When the feast was over, Tom explained to Nkoru how four members of his party had become lost. The witch doctor promised to send out search parties at once.

Meanwhile, Tom, Chow, and Akomo were escorted back to their camp. Tom's feelings were mixed when he discovered that Creel and one of the native porters had already returned.

"We got separated from Bud and the other bearer when we were chasing the peacock," Creel reported. "But don't worry—I'm sure they'll turn up safely tomorrow. Incidentally, the whole thing was a washout. We never got a single picture."

Chow growled angrily at Creel for ever having gone off on a "wild-goose chase." Tom said little, but inwardly he was seething with worry.

An anxious night of waiting followed. Next morning as they were eating breakfast, Tom sprang up with a shout of relief when a party of giant Wanguru tribesmen came trudging up to the camp. Bud and the other porter were with them!

Bud looked pale and shaken. "Wait'll I tell you what I saw, Tom!" he gasped. "You'll never believe me!"

CHAPTER IX

TALKING DRUMS

BUD was wild-eyed, and his khaki shirt and shorts were badly torn.

"Relax, pal." Tom smiled. "We'll believe you, but have something to eat first."

"Stop acting as if I'm goofy!" Bud roared. "We saw a dinosaur!"

"A dinosaur!" Tom's jaw dropped open. "You're kidding."

"You heard me—we saw a dinosaur!" Bud's face flushed with excitement as the words came pouring out. "The thing came blundering up to our camp last night. Just about scared us green. Tom, that thing was as big as a house! Long neck —head like an overgrown lizard. Jumpin' jets! When I saw that face zooming down at us from between the trees, I nearly went up in smoke!"

The native porter nodded his head vigorously.

"We cleared out—but fast," Bud reported. "We were afraid it was going to come after us—maybe trample us or gulp us down for a midnight snack. But it didn't. We could hear the—the thing clumping around in the brush and then it went away."

As he listened to the weird story, Darcy Creel became almost as agitated as Bud. "I told you there were reports of huge animals in this jungle!" he burst out. "What's more, they tie in with other stories about a large reptilian creature that exists in the lakes and rivers of the Central African rain forest—terrain almost identical with this."

"Wait a minute. Let's not go off the deep end about this," Tom said cautiously. "Where'd you hear these rumors about a big reptile?"

"They're in zoological literature."

"Did any of the writers ever *see* one of these monsters?" Tom asked.

Creel scowled. "Well—no. But their reports were based on good evidence."

Tom grew thoughtful. Bud's story of a gigantic animal "as big a house" had suddenly reminded the young inventor of Professor Eldreth and his "growth-process" theories mentioned by the museum curator. Was there really something in the Ngombian jungle that could make living creatures grow to gigantic size? The seven-foot Wanguru tribesmen were certainly above average!

"We don't even know if this *was* a dinosaur that Bud saw," Tom said aloud.

"Then what was it?" Bud countered.

"Let's track the creature," Creel pleaded.

"Obimbi and I tried to after daylight," Bud said, referring to his native companion. "From the looks of the underbrush, the creature must have gone into a creek or river that flowed close to our camp. Then, after these big fellows picked us up, I wanted to search for the spot where it came out —if it did come out—but they wouldn't let us."

"Why not?" Creel glanced at the Wangurus.

"As far as Obimbi could make out, it was taboo to go poking around any deeper into the forest."

Tom turned to the giant tribesmen. "Please ask them if they know anything about this big animal that our friends saw," he requested Akomo.

When the guide translated Tom's question, the Wangurus' eyes flashed fearfully. One of the warriors grunted a hasty reply.

"He says no—they know nothing about it."

"Will they help us track it down?" Tom persisted.

At this question, the Wangurus seemed even more upset. Their reply to Akomo was in the negative. When Creel quizzed them, they shrugged and answered evasively.

"More of that taboo business," Creel said, irritated. "We don't need their help, anyhow—we have our own boys. I vote we hunt for the creature as soon as Bud and Obimbi get a bite to eat!"

Tom shook his head. "We'd better not."

"But why not?" Creel retorted angrily. "This could be the biggest zoological find in years!"

"We're here on an urgent project for the Ngombian government, and it won't help if we antagonize the natives," Tom pointed out. "I'd like to find that dinosaur too, but we'll have plenty of opportunity later, when construction gets underway. For now, I think I've learned all I need to know about this jungle terrain."

The Wangurus were invited to share the camp breakfast. Before they left to return to their own village, Tom loaded them down with trade goods. Then Tom ordered Akomo and his bearers to strike camp.

"We're heading back to Imbolu," the young inventor announced.

On the way, Tom made several soil borings, in order to determine the ground structure of the rain forest. By noon the next day the party had arrived at Imbolu in their long native canoes.

"Welcome back!" Hank Sterling shouted.

He and the other crewmen from the *Sky Queen* rushed down to the riverbank. "By the way, skipper," Hank added, "we're still dying to know what that tom-tom jam session was for."

Tom chuckled and explained. Then he boarded the Flying Lab and radioed a report to the government ministry at Princetown. The young inventor added that he planned to take off in an hour for an aerial survey of the proposed highway route to East Ngombia, and then leave for the United States.

The Americans were just finishing lunch when Kwanu called back from the capital. Tom hurried to the flight compartment to take the message.

"Do you plan to land in the eastern province?" Kwanu inquired.

"We can if necessary, sir," Tom replied.

"Then you are invited to visit the headquarters of Afro-Metals, Limited," Kwanu went on. "The manager of the firm, Mr. Hans Macklin, would like you and your party to be his guests."

"Please tell him we'd be delighted." Tom was glad of a chance to learn more about the company which had been granted the mining concession to Ngombia's mineral resources. Perhaps he could pick up a clue to the mysterious plotters trying to balk his African venture.

Lunch over, the crew prepared for immediate takeoff. Soon the *Sky Queen* rose on its jet lifters and winged eastward over the jungle.

Viewed from the sky, the rain forest looked like a vast, billowing ocean of green. The tree crowns bulged like cauliflower clumps. Here and there taller giants thrust above the canopy in lonely splendor. Pink and orange liana blossoms and the lighter-colored flowers of the trees themselves flecked the greenery.

"Doesn't look as if you can make much of a ground survey from up here," Bud remarked.

"At least we know what it's like underneath," Tom said.

Midway on the flight, the boys noticed that the green forest canopy was broken by a belt of treeless, blackish terrain. It stretched north and south in a threadlike scar across the jungle.

"There's the swamp that stymied Burlow!" Tom exclaimed.

Hank and Creel came forward to the flight compartment as Tom swooped low to examine the queer gash. An updraft of hot air buffeted the plane. The swampy soil below seemed to be seething as if from some underground disturbance.

"What do you suppose is causing it?" Hank asked. "A volcanic break in the ground crust?"

Tom studied the terrain through binoculars. "Maybe—but it's different from anything I've ever heard of." Tom added to Creel, "How about you, Darcy? Any dope on the subject?"

Creel shook his head. "I've seen plenty of jungle swamps, but nothing like this."

"Want to go down and investigate?" Bud queried Tom.

The young inventor was thoughtful for several moments. "No, I guess there's no use wasting time on it right now, Bud," he said at last. "Just from looking at it, I'd say Burlow is right—that gunk would never support a conventional roadbed."

"Then what's the answer, genius boy?"

Tom shrugged. "Find a way to leapfrog over it, maybe. I'm still hoping to come up with some kind of aerial angle on this project. We don't have the *time* to hack a ground road through this whole wilderness if we want to wrap the job up in a short time."

Resuming their flight, the party soon landed at Copperville in East Ngombia. Here the jungle gave way to rolling savanna, sloping upward to forested highlands still farther beyond.

Copperville itself was a grimy town of iron-roofed huts on the shore of a river. A pall of smoke from the refinery darkened the scene. Farther inland lay a gaping open-pit mine where power shovels and antlike figures were at work.

Cars were waiting to take the Americans to the offices of Afro-Metals, Limited. Hans Macklin, the manager, greeted them. He was a thickset, reddish-haired man of late middle age.

"I've heard a great deal about the Swifts' scientific feats," he told Tom. "If your engineering skill can link our two provinces, it will be a great boon to Ngombia."

The visitors were shown through the vast mine workings and the ore-processing plant.

"Is copper your main export?" Tom asked.

Macklin nodded. "So far—but the mineral wealth of this country has hardly been tapped. We have placer gold mining upriver, and valuable deposits of manganese, columbite, and platinum."

"How is the ore shipped out?" Tom inquired.

"In very crude fashion—carried a long distance in baskets on the men's shoulders to the end of a road and put in trucks. If and when the highway is built, of course, it will go directly to Princetown and Ngombia's other ports."

That evening, Tom and his companions had dinner with some of the mining company's staff at Macklin's palatial, palm-shaded villa. Macklin—looking like a British empire builder with his

white dinner jacket and toothbrush mustache—
inquired about Tom's plans.

"Burlow Engineering is a highly experienced
outfit," Tom admitted. "Frankly, I doubt if I
could better their bid on a regular highway."

"How do you propose to tackle the project?"

"I still don't know. I'd thought about some kind
of atomicar transport system. But now that I've
seen your mining operation, I doubt if a fleet of
atomicars could handle your tonnage—and it
wouldn't help the tribesmen, either."

Changing the subject, Tom mentioned the dino-
saurlike animal Bud had seen. He also questioned
his host about the stretch of dark, seething terrain.
Macklin could offer no explanation of either mystery.

"The Ngombian jungle is so forbidding it has
never been properly explored," he told Tom.

After dinner, Tom took a stroll outdoors with
his host to enjoy the cool of the evening. Nearby,
the jungle loomed dark and green in the moon-
light. Tom's ears caught the beat of drums.

"The jungle telegraph," Tom remarked curiously. "Can you understand what it's saying, sir?"

Macklin listened. As the rhythmic beat continued, his face took on a startled look.

"That's odd," he murmured. "The drums are
saying that a terrible fate awaits the young white
juju man who has come to pierce the tabooed
jungle. *None must help him on fear of death!*"

CHAPTER X

SENSATIONAL NEWS

IN SPITE of himself, Tom felt a chill of fear at the eerie drum message.

"I say"—Macklin hesitated—"are you quite sure you want to take on this highway project?"

"Certainly. Why not?" Tom's voice sounded more confident than he felt at that moment.

Macklin frowned and fingered his mustache. "You may be taking on a more troublesome project than you realize. Perhaps even—dangerous."

He gave the young inventor a look of concern.

"Somebody has already tried pretty hard to stop me," Tom said. He told his host about the mysterious events that had taken place before he had left Shopton. Tom added bluntly, "Any idea who might be behind the trouble, sir?"

"East Ngombia is full of political hotheads," Macklin said worriedly. "Many of the local tribesmen would like to break away from the central government at Princetown and make this a separate country. Since your highway would bind the two provinces closer together, they may feel it's a threat to their plans."

"So they'll go all out to stop me?"

"Exactly. Now, perhaps, you can understand why I say this project may be dangerous."

Later that night, aboard the *Sky Queen,* Tom reported his conversation with Macklin to Bud.

"The drum business sure sounds weird," Bud said uneasily.

"It does, provided Macklin translated the message right."

Bud shot a glance at the young inventor. "Do you think he was lying?"

Tom shrugged. "He *might* have been trying to scare me off."

At that moment Darcy Creel walked into the bunk compartment. Tom turned to him casually and asked, "Did you understand what those jungle tom-toms were signaling tonight?"

"Tom-toms?" Creel looked surprised. "Sorry, but I don't think I heard them. Why?"

"Just wondered." Tom yawned and stretched out on his bunk, trying not to show any suspicion.

He was almost sure that he had noticed Creel outside the villa while the drums were sounding. Still, Creel might have paid no attention to the tom-toms, the young inventor realized.

Next morning the *Sky Queen* streaked homeward across the Atlantic. As the huge ship made its descent toward the American coast, a helicopter came gliding out to meet them.

"Sky Queen, this is helicopter two-one-six. Are you reading me?"

Tom responded into his microphone. "Reading you loud and clear."

"Helicopter to *Queen.* Will you please stop and allow someone to come aboard?"

Tom was startled by the request. "Who is this?" he demanded. "What's your business?"

"I'm just a commercial pilot, Mr. Swift," came the reply, "but my passenger says it's urgently important that he see you right away, before you land. His name is Corcoran."

Tom and Bud exchanged puzzled glances. "It could be a trick," Bud muttered.

Tom, however, was curious. After quizzing the helicopter pilot, the young inventor decided that they could safely agree to the request. So the *Sky Queen* slowed to a halt and descended to an altitude of five hundred feet on her jet lifters. The helicopter then hovered directly over the giant jet and dropped a rope ladder.

A bareheaded young man in slacks and sport jacket climbed down the ladder and scrambled in through the *Queen's* side hatch. Hank Sterling and another crewman helped him aboard. They searched the stranger for hidden weapons, then conducted him forward to the flight compartment.

"I'm a reporter for Consolidated Press," Corcoran told Tom and Bud. They shook hands.

"What did you want to see me about?" Tom asked.

"Actually, it's your friend I want to see," Corcoran said. Turning to Bud, he went on, "I'm empowered to offer you a thousand dollars for an exclusive eyewitness account of the dinosaur you saw in Africa."

"*What!*" Bud gaped in surprise.

"You heard me. A thousand bucks. I have a check right here—all made out."

Bud reddened. "L-look," he stammered, "I don't know how you got the word on this, but—"

"Report from West Africa," Corcoran explained tersely. "All the wire services picked it up. You're front-page news this morning, fella!"

"Well, my answer is no!" Bud snapped.

Corcoran looked irritated. "If it's more dough you want, maybe I can up the figure to twelve-fifty. But that's absolutely the—"

"The answer's still no!"

The reporter started to argue, but Tom cut him short. He explained that such a story, with no proof to back it up, might be damaging to the scientific prestige of Swift Enterprises.

"But the story's true, isn't it?"

"True or not, it could make us a laughing-stock," Tom retorted. "Now, if you'll please excuse us, we have to get back to Swift Enterprises."

Angrily, Corcoran left the ship and transferred to his rented helicopter. When the *Sky Queen* landed at the Enterprises airfield, it became clear why the reporter had been so eager to get a scoop. A swarm of newsmen were on hand, clamoring to interview Tom and his party. The young inventor gave them a brief statement.

"While we were in the jungle, one of our group sighted a large animal which has not yet been identified," he told the reporters. When a reporter asked if the animal looked like a dinosaur, Tom smiled noncommittally. "Sorry, no comment."

Mr. Swift and Harlan Ames were waiting at the *Queen*'s underground hangar.

"I thought we had better let you deal with the press as you saw fit, son," Mr. Swift explained, as he gripped Tom's hand warmly.

Tom told them the whole story. "Do you think I was right, Dad, in refusing to give any details?"

"Absolutely," Tom Sr. agreed. "Scientists the world over would condemn us for issuing such a sensational yarn without supporting evidence."

"The question is, how did the story leak out?" Ames said. "Any idea, skipper?"

Tom shook his head. "Not a clue, Harlan." He explained that the only person to whom he had mentioned the incident was Hans Macklin.

"I'll check back with him," Ames promised. "And the news wire services, too."

The security chief hurried to his office and phoned Consolidated Press in New York. The editor informed Ames that the story had originated in a cable dispatch from Lagos, Nigeria.

"Will you please check with your correspondent there—at our expense—and try to pin down the source?" Ames requested. "It's important."

"Okay, but it may take a while."

Next, Ames placed an overseas telephone call to Hans Macklin in Copperville. After half an hour of waiting, the call was routed through.

"I assure you, I never breathed a word of the story to anyone," Macklin told Ames. "Of course, others at the dinner may have overheard it. I'll try to find out and let you know."

Ames continued his probe. When he reported to Tom later, he looked disgusted. "The story came from some white big-game hunter who'd just flown out of Ngombia," Ames said. "Nobody got his name. He claimed to have heard about it from natives."

"A phony probably." Tom scowled thoughtfully. "Sounds to me like another move by our unknown enemy, Harlan."

"Sure—to make Swift Enterprises look ridiculous," Ames agreed. "If our scientific reputation were smeared, the Ngombian government might not want to entrust us with the highway project. Good thing you killed the story, skipper."

"I still think the leak must have come from Macklin's setup," Tom mused. "What do you know about Macklin, by the way?"

Ames shrugged. "Not much. He got his start in the South African gold fields. Pretty hard-boiled, they say, but a very smooth and efficient manager. I'll keep checking on him."

At noon Ned Newton came over from the construction plant to discuss the highway project with the Swifts and to hear Tom's report on his African survey trip.

"If atomicars won't do, what's the answer?"

Mr. Newton asked when Tom concluded the report.

"So far, I don't have an answer, Uncle Ned. But somehow we must find a way to shortcut the usual highway-construction methods. Otherwise, I don't see how we can beat Burlow's bid."

The telephone rang. Tom answered and the caller turned out to be his sister Sandy.

"Dr. Livingstone, I presume?" she said with a giggle. "Phyl and I were just wondering if we could snag you two African explorers for a dance at the Shopton Yacht Club tomorrow night."

Tom laughed. "Bud's not here, Sis, but I'll answer for both of us—it's a date."

As Tom hung up, Chow wheeled a food cart into the office and began serving lunch for the trio. In place of his chef's hat, the Texan was sporting a white ten-gallon hat.

"Say! That's a whole new outfit you have on, isn't it, Chow?" Mr. Swift asked admiringly.

"Sure is, boss—hat, shirt, britches—even spang-new hand-tooled boots. Some o' my ole range buddies sent 'em to me to wear on the big African job." Chow strutted about proudly to display his gaudy, new Western apparel. "I been walkin' on air ever since I tried 'em on!"

The cook stopped suddenly and stared at Tom, whose eyes glinted with excitement.

"Somethin' wrong, son?"

"Wrong?" Tom slapped the roly-poly chef on

the back so hard Chow's knees almost buckled. "Far from it, old-timer! When you said you were walking on air, you gave me a red-hot idea! . . . Dad, I've just figured how to lick our whole problem. Instead of running a road through the jungle, we'll build an *aerial* highway above the treetop level!"

Both Mr. Swift and Mr. Newton were astonished.

"I'm afraid I don't follow you, son."

Tom went on enthusiastically, "By running the highway above the trees, we can sidestep the mess of hacking a route through the jungle!"

"Great, but how do you intend to support this aerial highway?" put in Uncle Ned. "It certainly can't float in the air!"

"That's just exactly what it *will* do," Tom explained. "The roadway will be made of strong but featherweight material, supported in mid-air by repelatron beams—the same kind of repulsion rays used in my moon ship and atomicars!"

Grabbing pencil and paper, Tom pushed back the luncheon dishes and began sketching out his idea. The rays to hold up the highway would be generated by repelatron transmitters, planted at widely spaced intervals. Installing these would be a much cheaper and easier job than building a continuous highway through the jungle.

"A breath-taking idea, son," Mr. Swift commented. "The question is, can it be worked out?"

"Dad, I'm positive it can!"

"What about that swamp you described—the problem that stumped Burlow?" Ned Newton put in.

"I agree with him that it wouldn't take a conventional roadbed, Uncle Ned. But a few ray transmitters are a different matter. I see no reason why we can't plant those on pilings or concrete floats. Or, if necessary, we can freeze the gunk to make a temporary caisson and insert some solid fill."

Tom felt so confident that he plunged into work that afternoon on the job of inventing a suitable roadway material. He decided to use Durafoam—an air-celled adaptation of his amazing vacuum-celled Durabuoy plastic. This would be reinforced with fibers of Durastress, the fantastically strong and rigid material he had invented to contain his midget atomic dynamo.

By late the next day Tom had rigged a machine in his laboratory to produce the stuff. It jetted out the Durafoam bubbles into a long, dome-shaped, transparent plastic chamber where they were mixed with the fibers. Tom noticed that the jet nozzles, located on the far wall, were clogging.

"Good grief!" he muttered in disgust. "I'll have to wade through that goo and clean them out."

Donning plastic coveralls and rubber boots, he climbed a ladder and opened the inspection hatch, high in the dome wall. Tom stepped through and dropped to the concrete floor. The "mix" was already waist-high. The young inventor had to plow his way with difficulty through the sticky substance, but gradually worked himself into position to examine the nozzles. Standing a few feet away, he cleaned out the nozzles with a wire, then readjusted the size of the apertures.

"Whew! I guess that does it," Tom said to himself. "They seem to be spouting okay now."

Tom tried to turn and make his way to the hatch again. To his horror, he could scarcely move!

"The stuff's hardening!" he realized.

For several moments Tom floundered helplessly, fighting down a growing sense of panic. It was no use—the plastic foam was "setting" as firmly as cement! He was trapped!

"Help!" Tom yelled. Again and again he shouted until his throat was hoarse. No one answered.

Fear gripped him as he realized that it was long past quitting time. No one was within earshot. Meanwhile, the machine was running at full power, continuing to pump Durafoam—and the controls were outside the mixing chamber, far beyond reach!

In minutes he would be completely entombed in the plastic foam!

CHAPTER XI

A WEIRD MONSTER

SUMMONING all his willpower, Tom fought to steady his nerves. It was the colder air from outside the chamber, he realized, that was causing the mix to set.

"What a blockhead I was, not to close the hatch after I climbed in!" Tom thought.

If only he could reach the inspection door and shut it, he might be able to halt the hardening process. With a tremendous effort, Tom stretched out his arms. No use—the door was out of reach.

As another thought struck him, Tom began turning the jet nozzles to make the apertures smaller. This would slow down the output, but Tom realized that he dare not adjust them too finely. If the nozzles clogged again, the whole machine might explode from the back pressure!

By this time, the plastic foam was chest-high and hardening almost instantly. Tom was finding it difficult to breathe. He squirmed his shoulders, trying desperately to enlarge his body space. His skin was clammy as he felt himself giving way again to panic.

Suddenly Tom heard the door of the laboratory being opened.

"Tom!—Tom? Are you here?" It was his father!

The boy's throat felt so dry and tight that it was a moment before he could make any sound come out. "Dad!" he croaked. "I'm—inside—the—machine!"

"Great Scott!" the elder scientist gasped. He dashed across the laboratory and switched off the motor. "What happened, son?"

"Th-the Durafoam hardened, Dad. Get a solvent —you know the formula."

Mr. Swift hurried to a shelf of chemicals, selected a huge glass bottle, then returned and began pouring its contents slowly into the mixing chamber. Minutes passed as the liquid filtered down through the hard but porous Durafoam, dissolving the material layer by layer. At last it had softened enough for Tom to move about in the slush. He made his way to the hatch, and his father's strong arms reached in to pull him through the opening.

"Whew!" Tom was panting and shivering. He was still caked with the whitish, oozing Durafoam. "Th-thanks, Dad."

Mr. Swift helped him out of his coveralls and boots, then grinned and gave Tom a reassuring hug. "Better sit down and get your breath, son. I'll bring you a glass of water."

After a few moments Tom was able to talk about

his terrible experience. He explained how the mishap had occurred. Then he smiled. "Dad, that Durafoam hardens even faster than I had expected. I'd better mix in a little chemical retardant when I use the stuff for my highway-laying process."

Mr. Swift was keenly interested in the progress of Tom's newest scientific undertaking. The young inventor explained that his plastic highway would be laid—or rather extruded—by a hovering slow-skimming aircraft. For this job, he planned to use one of his new graphicopters, which were already being produced and sold by the Swift Construction Company.

The two Toms were deep in their discussion when Mr. Swift suddenly exclaimed, "Good night! I almost forgot why I dropped over here. I happened to call home, and Sandy asked me to rout you out of your lab so you wouldn't be late for your double date this evening."

Tom grinned sheepishly. "I forgot, too," he admitted. "Good old Sandy! She saved my life."

After driving home with his father, Tom showered and changed. By the time he came downstairs, in a white shirt, bow tie, sport jacket, and slacks, Bud had already arrived and was chatting with Sandy in the living room.

"Boy! Whoever said you have to wait for *girls* to get dressed for a date?" But wisecracked, with a glance at his wristwatch.

"He'd probably still be deep in some experiment if I hadn't reminded him," Sandy pouted.

"I was pretty deep, at that—practically up to my chin, in fact." Tom chuckled but did not explain, since he always preferred not to recount his dangerous experiences for fear of alarming Sandy and his mother.

After saying good-by to Mr. and Mrs. Swift, the three piled into Bud's red convertible and sped off to pick up Phyl Newton. Ten minutes later they arrived at the Shopton Yacht Club on Lake Carlopa.

The two couples enjoyed a gay dinner on the terrace overlooking the water. They were just about to start dancing when a white-jacketed steward paged Bud by name.

"Phone call in the reception room, sir," he explained when Bud beckoned him to the table.

Bud excused himself and went to the telephone. A muffled voice answered.

"Is this Mr. Bud Barclay?"

"Speaking."

"With regard to the—er—strange, large animal you saw in Africa"—the caller spoke in a faintly foreign accent—"I may be able to provide you with some important scientific information on the subject. Are you interested?"

Bud was mystified, but felt his pulse stirring with excitement. "I might be. Why? Who is this?"

"My name does not matter. If you will come to 104 River Road at once, I will give you the information."

"But wait a minute! I still want to know wh—" Bud broke off as he heard the receiver click at the other end of the line.

He hurried back to the table and told Tom and the girls about the call. "Of course, it may be some nut," he ended, "but I'd sure like to find out."

Sandy's blue eyes widened with alarm. "Oh, Bud," she exclaimed, "please don't! It may be a trap!"

Phyl, too, expressed concern.

"What do you think, Tom?" Bud asked.

"I don't know. We could call the police and let them check first, I suppose."

"That might scare off our informant," Bud pointed out. "Even if all this is on the level, the man must have some reason for keeping under cover or he would have come to see me."

Tom nodded thoughtfully. "Suppose the two of us go together—but I'll call Ames first. That is, if the girls don't mind waiting for us."

Seeing that the boys were determined, both Sandy and Phyl begged to be taken along. Tom and Bud, however, flatly refused to risk their safety. After the boys had promised to be cautious and to return as quickly as possible, the girls agreed to wait for them at the yacht club.

Tom and Bud hurried to the reception room, where Tom paused long enough to call Harlan Ames. He told the security chief about the mysterious telephone message and added, "If I don't report back to you by nine-thirty, Harlan, get the police and come after me."

Ames hesitated uneasily. "Sure you're doing the right thing, skipper?"

"Let's say I think it's worth taking a chance. If our enemy's tied in on this deal, we might pick up a good lead."

"Okay. But please, Tom—watch your step."

"Don't I always?"

Ames snorted. "That's a laugh!"

Chuckling, Tom hung up. The boys dashed out to the parking lot and climbed into Bud's convertible. He sped off with a spurt of gravel.

When they turned into River Road, Bud manipulated his spotlight to pick out the house numbers. The homes in this area were all old mansions with spacious grounds.

Presently Bud saw the number 104 on a brick fence pillar. He swung up the drive. The glare of the headlights revealed a huge, Victorian-era frame house, shuttered and silent. Bud stopped the car and they got out.

"Looks empty from here," Bud murmured.

"It *is* empty—there's a 'for sale' sign," Tom pointed out.

The grounds were wooded with eerie-looking pines and hemlocks, and the tall grass was thickly overgrown with weeds. Tom shone his pocket flashlight as they began prowling about, searching for signs of their mysterious informant.

Bud chuckled nervously. "Maybe the whole thing was just a—"

He broke off and both boys stiffened with sudden shock. *A weird, long-necked monster, resembling a miniature brontosaurus, came stalking out of the trees straight toward them!*

CHAPTER XII

CHOW'S SKYWAY MISHAP

"J-J-JUMPIN' jets!" Bud's voice came out in a hoarse whisper. "Do you see what I see?"

"I see it, all right," Tom replied, "but I don't believe it!"

The boys' eyes bulged at the fantastic sight. The creature was too far away in the darkness to be clearly revealed by Tom's small beam, but they could see its neck weaving from side to side as it advanced. An eerie screech from the monster sent chills racing down their spines.

As it emerged from the shadow of the trees, Tom sucked in his breath. Something about the creature had stirred a suspicion in his mind. But before he could speak, a flash of brilliant light blinded the boys momentarily.

The next second there was a deafening outburst of shrieks, hoots, and yells! Figures burst from the trees and shrubbery!

Voices cried, *"Did you see Tom's and Bud's*

faces?" . . . *"Man, oh man! They fell for that one all right!"*

Tom and Bud were still blinking and gaping when another flash bulb exploded. As the boys' eyes adjusted to the glare, they saw half a dozen of their teen-age pals surrounding them—roaring with laughter!

"Rock Harriman!" Bud groaned as he spotted the pudgy figure of Shopton High's all-star tackle. Rock was famous for his practical jokes. "We should have known!"

Meanwhile, the "monster" was coming apart. It turned out to be two youths in a masquerade horse costume. A long papier-mâché neck and dinosaur head had been mounted over it.

"Dick Hempstead and Harry Ellers!" Tom chuckled ruefully as he recognized them. "I thought that tiny head and long neck looked familiar, but I couldn't place the hind legs."

Rock waved his camera triumphantly. "Boy, just wait'll I develop these pictures of you guys!" he crowed. "I think I'll send the first one to the newspapers—a follow-up to that 'Boy Meets Dinosaur' story!"

Bud's face reddened. "Okay, okay—don't rub it in. I suppose you were the wise guy who called me at the yacht club, too?"

"Yup. The whole thing was a stroke of genius, if I do say so myself." Rock and his cohorts gave way to another outburst of mirth.

Tom laughed in spite of himself. "We bit, all

right—hook, line, and sinker. Now that you've pulled your gag, how about rounding up some dates and joining us at the yacht club?"

Tom's suggestion was hailed with cheers. After the pranksters had picked up some friends, the group drove to the club where Sandy and Phyl were still waiting.

"We unearthed a live dinosaur out on River Road," Bud explained to the two girls, "so Tom decided to throw a party to celebrate."

The evening proved a huge success. When it was over, Rock Harriman unloaded his camera and thrust the roll of film into Tom's hand.

"Here's a present," Rock said. "You fellows were such good sports, I'll let *you* decide what to do with those pictures I took."

Tom grinned with relief. "We'll frame 'em."

On Monday morning Tom called Hank Sterling and Arv Hanson into his laboratory. Arv was one of the Swifts' most trusted craftsmen. He often worked on the pilot models of Tom's inventions.

"Here's the info on the repelatron transmitters for my aerial highway," Tom said, showing them some sketches. "The transmitters will be spaced at half-mile intervals. I'll need half a dozen built for my pilot test."

The transmitter units would stand about ten feet high. Each one had a bell-shaped base. From this, a column arose which flared into a fan-shaped opening at the top.

"Let's take it part by part," Tom said. "Down

in this bell-shaped housing at the bottom is one of my midget atomic dynamos. It will generate the power for the transmitter."

Tom went on to explain that just above this, inside the column, was the electronic apparatus of the repelatron itself.

"The rays which support the highway," Tom continued, "will be beamed out through this fanlike opening at the top. They'll sweep back and forth thousands of times per second—spreading out in a wide enough arc to support a half-mile span of the highway."

"What about these tubes sticking out on each side of the unit?" Hank put in.

"They'll project rays to the right and left of the highway. And these rays will be reflected back toward the highway, so as to lock it rigidly in position and keep the span from swaying from side to side."

"How are the rays reflected?" Arv asked.

Tom produced another set of drawings. "By means of these twin-horned reflectors. They'll be bracketed to trees that have been trimmed."

The sweep beams, Tom concluded, would support the highway at an elevation of over two hundred feet—enough to clear the highest trees.

"A real jungle skyway!" Hank said admiringly.

Tom grinned. "That gives me an idea, Hank—let's call this a repelatron skyway."

"Good name. We'll get right to work on these transmitter units."

Meanwhile, Tom went off to the hangar to convert one of his graphicopters for the road-laying operation. The foam plastic would be pumped out through a road-width slot along the base of the copter's storage tank.

Chow, who had come in, watched Tom weld a part of the graphicopter assembly in place. He asked about the newfangled road layer.

"It'll squirt out the highway as if we were squeezing it out of a giant toothpaste tube," Tom explained.

"Brand my bridgework, that's plumb *re*markable." Chow looked awed. "You ain't fixin' to squirt out the whole highway in one swoop?"

"No. The graphicopter will only hold enough mix to lay about half a mile per load. But each section will bond automatically to the preceding span as the plastic hardens." Tom added, "I have two flying supply tanks on the drawing board— 'helitanks,' you might call them—for refilling the graphicopter in the air. They aren't built yet, so for my demonstration I'll refill from tank trucks on the ground."

Within a week, Tom was ready for a pilot test of his repelatron skyway. The transmitters had been set up along one wall of the four-mile-square Enterprises enclosure. A crowd of employees gathered to watch the demonstration.

"Boy, this'll really be something for you to write back to Texas about!" Bud remarked to Chow as they waited for the test to begin.

The cook's face twisted into a conspiratorial leer. "Confidentially, Buddy boy, ole Chow is goin' to have the honor o' bein' the first hombre to walk on Tom's floatin' highway!"

Bud turned in surprise. "How come?"

"Jest watch an' see, son." The stout cook stomped off with a sly chuckle.

Bud was puzzled, but soon forgot Chow's boast as Tom came soaring into view from the airfield in his converted graphicopter. The young inventor hovered down to the precise height of the test skyway and lined up on the row of transmitters. Then he began to fly forward slowly, pouring out the plastic roadway in the copter's wake.

A murmur of amazement went up from the spectators—then cheers when they saw the flat white ribbon of highway floating in the air without visible support. The repelatron rays held it firmly at the height of a ten-story building.

"Wow!" Bud gasped to Arv Hanson. "I'd like to see Burlow Engineering or anyone else top that for a road-paving demonstration!"

The whole span was almost completed when Arv suddenly tugged Bud's arm.

"Hey, what's that? Part of the show?"

A small aerial platform—one of the "flying carpets," or "repelatron donkeys," which Tom had designed for short-haul transport work on the moon—was sailing toward the scene of the demonstration. A pudgy figure in a cowboy hat could be seen perched atop the platform.

"Good grief!" Bud exclaimed. "It's Chow!"

The cook maneuvered his flying carpet alongside and stepped boldly out onto the skyway. The crowd broke into laughing applause as Chow waved his hat and began walking across the span.

But the next moment the cheers gave way to gasps of alarm. Evidently the plastic had not fully hardened—Chow's boots were sinking deep into the still-soft material! The spectators could see him teetering wildly, trying to extricate his legs from the gooey mass. But his frantic efforts only worsened the situation—in seconds he sank up to his knees!

"He'll fall through!" Arv cried in horror.

"Won't the rays hold him up?" Bud asked.

"Not a chance! The transmitters are only tuned to repel the highway material!"

"Help! Help!" Chow screamed.

The workmen and spectators milled in panic, vainly seeking some way to catch the stout cook when he plunged downward. In the nick of time the graphicopter came swooping to the rescue, dangling its filler hose.

"Grab on!" Tom shouted.

Chow clutched frantically at the hose. The graphicopter rose, tugging him free from the sticky morass. Then it hovered down, clear of the skyway, and deposited him safely on the ground.

Chow stood quaking and trembling, his face gray with fright. Onlookers crowded around him.

"You know what they say, old-timer—'Fools

rush in where angels fear to tread,' " Bud wise-cracked.

"B-b-brand my sagebrush stew," Chow muttered, "I come doggone near *bein'* an angel!"

Tom looked somewhat chagrined as he landed. "I must have added too much chemical retardant to the mix," he explained to his father and Hank Sterling. "It slowed down the setting process too much—that's why the stuff is still mushy."

After taking Bud aloft to retrieve Chow's flying carpet, Tom hurried to his laboratory to prepare a new batch of Durafoam. By this time the highway had hardened. Hank reduced the power output of the transmitters so the span would sink low enough to be removed.

Two hours later Tom was ready for another test. This time, Bud accompanied him in the graphicopter. After laying a half-mile section of the skyway, Tom turned over the controls to his co-pilot and climbed out onto the floating pavement. The watching crowd held its breath as the young inventor took several tentative steps, then applauded. The Durafoam had hardened perfectly.

"Nice going, pal," Bud congratulated Tom as he climbed back aboard.

"You haven't seen anything yet!"

After completing the whole span, Tom steered the graphicopter in a downward glide to pave a sloping approach to the skyway. Then he landed, climbed into the cab of a heavy truck, and began driving it up the ramp. The paving was already solid! The onlookers gaped and broke into loud applause as they saw the truck reach the top of the ramp and continue out along the roadway, floating more than two hundred feet in the air! Tom waved down to the spectators jubilantly.

Later that afternoon, when the demonstration was over, Tom made a number of other strength tests of his skyway before dismantling it. He was interrupted as his father came speeding up in a jeep. Mr. Swift looked rather stunned.

"Tom, I've just seen something incredible!" he gasped. "Please come back to your lab with me at once!"

CHAPTER XIII

SUPERWORMS

"WHAT'S wrong, Dad?" Tom inquired eagerly.

"Son, in view of all the hubbub over Bud's dinosaur, I won't even try to describe the—the — Well, I prefer you to see this with your own eyes."

"Let's go!" Tom climbed into his father's jeep and they sped off toward the building which housed the young inventor's private laboratory.

When they arrived, Mr. Swift led the way to a storeroom on the first floor. He flung open the door, then turned to watch his son's reaction.

Tom gasped. Enormous brown worms—the size of huge snakes and as thick as a man's wrist—were wriggling and slithering about the shelves and over the equipment stacked on the floor!

"What in the name of science are they?" Tom murmured hoarsely.

"I was hoping you could tell *me*," Mr. Swift replied. "From the looks of them, they seem to be overgrown earthworms."

"Overgrown is right—they're more like baby boas!" Tom could hardly believe his eyes.

Suddenly an amazing thought struck him. "Wait a minute, Dad! I just had an idea!"

Tom dashed across the corridor to his private laboratory and called Chow Winkler on the plant intercom. The cook arrived moments later.

"Chow, didn't you mention something to me about leaving bait here at the lab?" Tom asked.

The roly-poly Texan nodded, looking puzzled at Tom's question. "Yup, I aim to go fishin' in Lake Carlopa, so I dug me up some nice juicy night crawlers the other evenin'. Why, boss?"

"Where did you leave those night crawlers?"

"Well, I come across some cans o' earth in your storeroom, so I stuck the worms in there to keep 'em fresh. I didn't think you'd mind."

Tom grinned wryly. "Take a look." He led the way to the storeroom and opened the door.

Chow started as if he had been stung, his eyes bulging at sight of the enormous worms. "Great hoppin' horned toads!" he gulped. "You mean the-the-these is *them?*"

"They are—if my hunch is correct," Tom said.

Mr. Swift looked as baffled as the cook. "What's your theory, son?" he asked.

"Dad, those cans of earth are the soil samples I brought back from the Ngombian jungle. Did you ever hear of a Professor Welkin Eldreth?"

Mr. Swift rubbed his chin thoughtfully. "Eldreth. *Hmm.* A biologist, wasn't he?"

Chow's eyes bulged at sight of the enormous worms

"That's right. And Dr. Gorde says Eldreth had some odd theories about a plant or mineral extract which could control the growth processes of living organisms. Dad, the place Professor Eldreth went to pursue his researches was *Ngombia!*"

Mr. Swift stared at his son. "You mean that the extract Eldreth was after is present in those soil samples?"

"Exactly. Some sort of growth-triggering mineral. The worms must have digested it, and this is the result!" Tom's eyes blazed with excited interest. "Professor Eldreth disappeared into the jungle twenty years ago—but this backs up his theories!"

Mr. Swift paced back and forth, frowning. "It seems incredible—yet we have the evidence right here before our eyes. I'd say Eldreth's ideas are worth looking into."

Tom immediately telephoned Miss Remple, the Enterprises librarian. He asked her to gather all the scientific journals in which Professor Eldreth's technical papers had appeared. That evening Tom and his father perused them avidly.

Both the Swifts had a keen grasp of all branches of science, including biology. They knew about recent research experiments in the growth field, such as polyploidy or chromosome multiplication—growth hormones—and DNA, the giant molecule which controls cell development. Judging by his writings, Eldreth seemed to have foreseen much of this work.

What caught Tom's eye, however, was an article about the breeding of "throwbacks"—animals which resembled earlier kinds. Professor Eldreth had claimed that extinct species of animals could be re-created by careful breeding of present-day animals to bring out the characteristics of the older beasts from which they were descended.

"Take a look at this, Dad." Tom handed the article to his father.

Mr. Swift read it rapidly. "Very interesting. Eldreth was certainly ahead of his time."

"He sure was! There's a fellow at the Munich Zoo in Germany who's re-created the aurochs, or prehistoric European cattle, after the species died out hundreds of years ago. He picked out cattle which showed some of the same characteristics as the older type and kept breeding them together until he produced a whole herd that are exactly like the ancient aurochs. And he has done the same with the wild horse."

Mr. Swift nodded. "Yes, I recall those experiments. The Irish wolfhound was brought back the same way. And a scientist at the University of Chicago once bred guinea pigs with so many toes that their feet resembled fins—just like their ancestors who lived in the seas ages ago."

Tom sat bolt upright. "Dad, this sounds so crazy I'm almost afraid to say it, but—"

"Go ahead, son."

"Well, that dinosaur Bud saw—or whatever it was—do you suppose Professor Eldreth could have been experimenting along the lines we've been talking about and produced such a creature?"

Mr. Swift got up from his chair and strode about the room, looking deeply thoughtful. "A man-made dinosaur!" he murmured. "Sounds fantastic, Tom, and yet—that could be the answer."

The Swifts decided to keep the whole weird idea to themselves for the time being. But they hoped that Tom might uncover more evidence when he returned to Ngombia.

Next morning Tom called the Ngombian Embassy in Washington and informed officials that he was ready to offer a solution to their highway problem. A date was set for a demonstration.

That afternoon Bud found Tom in the hangar machine shop, at work on the road-laying gear.

"What cooks, genius boy?" Bud inquired.

Tom explained that he was installing an extrusion die at each side of the pouring slot. "They'll form a small channel along each side of the highway. And as the road is laid, a continuous length of wire will be inserted in each channel, to provide the highway with guardrails."

"Guardrails! For what—ants?" Bud stared at his friend. "One wire on each side—and not even raised above the road surface. How can that protect anything from falling off?"

Tom chuckled. "Don't jump to conclusions, fly-boy. The wires won't *be* the guardrails—they'll *provide* the guardrails."

Tom took a pencil and sketched out his idea.

"You see, those wires will be transmitting antennas, connected to a repelatron generator for each side of the highway. The wires will project a curtain of repelatron rays upward from the road surface on each side. And since they'll be full-spectrum rays, capable of repelling all forms of matter, no vehicle or pedestrian will be able to break through the curtain."

The following week Kwanu and a number of other Ngombian officials arrived for the demonstration. They gasped as the highway took shape in mid-air, in the wake of Tom's skimming graphicopter. A sloping approach was laid at both ends of the span. Then the guardrail antenna wires were installed.

Next, a fleet of cars and trucks was driven over the skyway. Several of the drivers deliberately tried to ram their vehicles off the edge of the span— much to the Ngombians' horror. But cheers and applause followed when the audience saw how the ray curtain repelled them from danger.

"We are breathless with admiration!" Kwanu told the Swifts and Mr. Newton later.

"The credit belongs entirely to my son, sir," Mr. Swift replied. Tom reddened at their praise.

After studying the proposed contract for the jungle skyway, Kwanu promised to transmit it to his government at once. "But I can assure you the terms will be accepted," he added. "Not only have you slashed the time to a minimum—your price is far below Burlow's."

In the days that followed, Swift Enterprises hummed with activity. Tom worked night and day organizing the supplies, schedules, technical personnel, and equipment for the project.

The evening before the expedition was to take off, Sandy and Phyl gave a *bon voyage* masquerade party at the Swifts'. Tom, in a gorilla suit, grinned when he spotted a green Martian.

"Your pointed head gave you away, Bud," he joked.

"Listen, wise guy, that's my built-in radio antenna," Bud retorted.

Tom glanced around the room, chuckling at the costumes of the guests. "I'd hate to meet *that* on a dark night," he remarked, pointing to a skeleton figure who had just arrived. "Wonder how Chow will disguise his bay window!"

"He can always come as a circus fat lady," Bud suggested. "Say, I'll bet that walking palm tree over there is Darcy Creel."

Later, with the party in full swing, Tom was called to the phone. Harlan Ames was calling.

"Are your guests all masked?" Ames inquired.

"Masked and costumed both. Why?"

The security chief's voice was tense with alarm. "Tom, I've just received an anonymous tip that one of your guests is an impostor. He may be a killer who aims to stop you from carrying out your African project!"

CHAPTER XIV

THE SKELETON BOMBER

TOM stiffened at the news. "How did you get the tip, Harlan?" he asked softly.

"An unsigned note. I got home late and found it slipped under the door. No clues."

"Okay, don't do anything just yet," Tom told him. "Let me try to handle this."

After hanging up, Tom stood for a moment deep in thought. How could he check out the tip without alarming the guests or spoiling Sandy's party?

A few seconds later Tom strode off in search of his sister. Sandy, dressed in a leopard costume, was just putting on a new dance record.

"How many guests are here at the party, Sis?"

Sandy giggled. "At least a houseful! Why?"

"Just wondered. Did everyone show up?"

"Now that you mention it, I'm not sure. *Mm*— let me see. If you want to count Bud and Phyl, there should be twenty-four."

"Thanks." Tom went out on the patio and then came back inside, counting every guest in sight.

There were exactly twenty-four!

Tom frowned uneasily. Could Ames's tip have been a hoax? Or had the impostor overpowered and taken the place of one of the real guests?

Unfortunately, the Swifts' alarm system had been turned off for the evening, since some of the guests did not possess the special wristwatches. Sandy and Phyl had felt that with the grounds brightly illuminated, there would be no danger, especially since all the guests would be asked to show their invitations at the door. But Tom realized that the impostor might have used his victim's invitation.

"I'd better have everyone unmask—pronto! But even that would be risky," Tom reflected.

What if the intruder *was* a killer, as Ames feared? The scare of being detected might panic him into shooting, or into some other hasty action which would endanger the merrymakers.

Suddenly Tom remembered something. "That guest in the skeleton costume! I saw him earlier this evening, but not when I took the nose count! That would make twenty-five people in costume!"

To be sure he had made no mistake, Tom repeated his circuit of the patio and the first-floor rooms. Mr. Skeleton was nowhere in sight! With growing alarm, Tom slipped upstairs and glanced into room after room. Again he drew a blank.

There was only one place left to look—the basement. Tom switched on the light and darted down the steps, two at a time. He gasped as he glimpsed the black-and-white skeleton figure streaking toward one of the basement windows!

By the time Tom reached the bottom of the stairs, the man had already flung open the sash and was hoisting himself out.

The young inventor made a wild dash for the window, trying to grab the fugitive's legs. But the man kicked backward viciously. His heel caught Tom a jarring blow under the chin!

Stunned, Tom reeled backward. By the time he recovered, the skeleton had wriggled safely out.

"Help! Stop him, someone!"

Tom suddenly spotted the answer to the intruder's actions. A metal cylinder wired to a detonating device lay on the floor near the furnace! The man had been planting a bomb!

"Help! Catch the spy!" Tom shouted.

His yells were drowned by the blare of dance music from the patio. Tom hesitated frantically, torn between two choices. Should he go after the fleeing figure without bothering to disarm the bomb? But it might be set to explode any moment!

Turning back toward the furnace, Tom hastily disconnected the detonator. Then he followed the fugitive out the window. By now, his quarry was nowhere in sight. A short sprint across a lighted stretch of lawn had carried the "skeleton" safely off into the darkness. From the undisturbed dancing and smooth hum of conversation on the patio, it was evident that none of the guests had even noticed the intruder's dash to escape.

Still shaken and angry, Tom returned to the house. He telephoned Ames and filled him in. "Call the police right away," Tom said. "Maybe a scout car can spot the guy before he ditches his costume."

"Did he arrive in a car?" Ames asked.

"I don't know. But even behind a wheel that skeleton getup should be easy to spot."

"Okay, skipper—glad no one got hurt. And I'll send someone around for that bomb assembly."

"Thanks, Harlan!" After hanging up, Tom rejoined the festivities. The party continued gaily with no one but Tom aware of their narrow escape.

Next morning the Swift and Newton families drove to the Enterprises airfield to watch the expedition's departure. After receiving the Newtons' good wishes, Tom got a quick kiss each from Sandy and Phyl and embraced his mother. Then Tom Sr. gripped his son's hand warmly.

"It's a big undertaking, son," Mr. Swift murmured. "I'm confident you can handle it in a way that will bring credit to America."

"I'll try, Dad. Thanks—and so long!"

Minutes later, the *Sky Queen* zoomed aloft and seaward. Then three huge cargo jets took off.

As Tom streaked over the South Atlantic, a radio call came in from Harlan Ames.

"The skeleton bomber's been nabbed, skipper," he reported. "Happened early this morning upstate—I just got the word. A trooper chased a speeding car, made the driver pull over, and spotted the skeleton costume on the back seat."

"That's great, Harlan! Who is the fellow?"

"He's a hood named Willie Jarvel. So far he won't talk—but the costume fits him perfectly. By the way, guess how he carried that cylinder."

"How?"

"Inside one of the padded ribs sewn on the front of his suit. The padding had been removed. He's being brought to Shopton," Ames added. "I'll let you know if we get anything out of him."

Before noon, the air convoy landed in Ngombia. A car was waiting to whisk Tom to the Ministry of Economic Development. Here, Kwanu informed him that native work gangs had already been organized and were standing by at Imbolu and Copperville.

"I have also hired an experienced big-game hunter—an Englishman," Kwanu went on. "His name is Luke Auber. He will help you deal with the jungle tribesmen and protect your work crews from animal attack."

"Thanks. We can use him," Tom said.

As soon as he returned to the airport, the planes took off for Imbolu. When they landed, a tall, lean man strolled out from the village to meet them. Black-haired and deeply tanned, he was wearing jungle-stained khakis and a broad-brimmed felt hat.

"I'm Luke Auber," he told Tom.

They shook hands and Tom introduced him to

the others. Auber had a rather surly manner, which riled Bud. His cold-eyed, hard-bitten look stirred Bud's distrust. Suddenly he remembered hearing from Tom that the dinosaur story had been given out by a big-game hunter in Nigeria.

"Ever been in Nigeria?" Bud asked.

Auber nodded casually.

"How recently?"

Auber had already turned away, ignoring Bud's question. Later Chow tried to corner him for a friendly chat. Auber listened with a thin smile, looking the cook over and saying nothing.

"Bit blubbery for jungle work, aren't you, old boy?" he remarked when Chow paused for breath. "Oh, well, you'll soon sweat some off, I suppose."

Chow was left stuttering with indignation. "Brand my cactus hash, I don't trust that Limey!"

"Neither do I," put in Bud. "He could be the hunter who tipped off the newspapers."

Tom shrugged. "There's no real reason to suspect him—he's not the only hunter in Africa."

Darcy Creel came sauntering up. "Er—ahem— maybe I shouldn't say this," he confided, "but Auber doesn't have too good a reputation."

"How so?" Tom asked.

"For one thing, I've heard he's been in trouble over in Kenya—for ivory poaching, or mistreating natives." Creel spoke in a low voice.

Tom frowned. "Thanks. But since the Ngombian government hired Auber, I'm afraid I'll have to keep him on for the time being."

Soon a base camp with metal shacks had been set up at the village. Then Hank Sterling left with two of the cargo jets for Copperville in East Ngombia. After landing, Hank radioed back a precise navigational fix of the spot chosen for the eastern terminus.

Meanwhile, a skywriting graphicopter had been unloaded from the *Queen* and assembled for flight. Tom and Bud took off in it and began streaking a line of dye across the jungle vegetation.

"Pretty neat," Bud commented. "We won't even need a ground survey for the skyway, eh?"

Tom nodded. "We're painting the route as we fly," he explained. "Our automatic navigator is steering us on the shortest straight-line course between the two ends of the skyway."

With the route laid out, work began at once— Tom starting construction from the western end, Hank from the east. The following day, as work crews cleared the sites and poured the foundations, Tom lowered half a dozen repelatron transmitters into place by cable from the *Sky Queen*.

Next morning, as more transmitters were being readied for air-drop, Arv Hanson came striding back to camp. His face was white with anger.

"What's wrong?" Tom asked.

"Plenty!" Arv blurted out. "All those transmitters you planted yesterday have been wrecked!"

CHAPTER XV

NOCTURNAL RAIDERS

"WRECKED?" Tom stared in dismay.

Arv nodded grimly. "Deliberate sabotage. Wait'll you see, skipper—it's sickening."

Tight-lipped, Tom accompanied Hanson into the bush. The first transmitter was located only a short distance upriver from the village. Tom gasped in helpless rage at the sight that met his eyes.

The unit had been wrenched and toppled from its foundation. The repelatron-generating gear inside had been ripped out and smashed. The ground was strewn with electronic debris.

"Boy, would I like to sabotage the creeps who did this!" Tom clenched his fists bitterly.

"The other units all got the same treatment," Arv said. "Half a dozen transmitters shot!"

Tom was heartsick as the two hiked back to camp. Its metal shacks glittered in the vivid African sunlight, with the thatch-roofed houses of

Imbolu visible just beyond. Crewmen and natives stopped work as they saw Tom and Arv returning.

"Trouble?" Bud asked, noting their grim faces.

"Our enemy's back in business." Tom reported what had happened. Bud and the others were outraged.

Darcy Creel cleared his throat uncomfortably. "I—uh—don't like to say this," he murmured, "but I think it's my duty."

"Say what?" Tom stared at him.

"Well, I couldn't sleep last night, so I got up—and I noticed Luke Auber was gone from camp."

All eyes turned suspiciously on the hunter. Auber, who preferred to sleep in the open, had spent the night stretched out in a blanket by a campfire.

"Okay, what's your story?" Bud demanded.

The lean, tough-looking hunter grinned back sarcastically—his cold gray eyes emphasized by his deep tan. "Your friend Creel is quite right. I did leave camp."

"Why?" Tom asked.

"Noises," Auber replied. "It could have been those transmitters being smashed, I suppose. Anyhow, I went out to scout around."

Tom's eyes kindled. "What did you find?"

"Signs that someone else from our camp had already been out, meeting some strangers."

Auber's news provoked skeptical murmurs.

The hunter shrugged. "I didn't expect you to believe me. But come along and I'll show you."

He led the way, about two hundred yards from

camp, to where the river trail became fringed with dense jungle vegetation. At one point, a narrow passage had been forced through the dense undergrowth. It led to a tiny clearing in which the grass was crushed and trampled. From here another, wider path through the brush emerged from the forest. Evidently the strangers Auber had spoken of had come this way.

"Brand my runnin' iron, you sure read the sign right," Chow commented, squinting about.

"How do we know he didn't come here himself?" Bud muttered.

Auber plucked something from the grass. "Didn't notice this last night with my flashlight," he said. "Your brand, isn't it, Creel?"

He held out a half-smoked cigarette stub. Its paper bore the "Gold Coast" trademark. Creel's face turned flaming red.

"What are you trying to do, Auber—frame me?"

The hunter grinned. "I just asked a simple question."

" 'Gold Coast' is the most common brand sold in this part of Africa," Creel retorted. "Plenty of people smoke them. For that matter, you could have planted it here."

"Relax!" Tom broke in. "Accusing each other won't help. The important thing now is to repair the damage that's been done."

As they returned to camp, Bud asked quietly, "Which one do you believe, Tom?"

"It's a toss-up, Bud—either one could be lying.

But it sure looks as if the saboteurs met *someone* from our outfit!"

The damaged repelatrons were replaced and work continued. Next day a cargo jet arrived at Imbolu from Shopton—the first of a regular series of shuttle flights to keep the work crews supplied.

Tom had assigned Bud and Arv the job of planting the next group of transmitters from the *Sky Queen*. Meanwhile, Tom took off in a road-laying graphicopter to begin pouring the first sections of the skyway. This included an entrance ramp sloping upward from a point near the village.

The Ngombian workmen and villagers were goggle-eyed to see the white ribbon of roadway floating in thin air over the jungle trees. What impressed them most of all was the seemingly magical way Tom had spun the skyway out of his queer-shaped whirlybird. They began pointing him out in awed whispers and bowing low whenever he passed.

"Think they'll have nerve enough to use your skyway when it's done?" Bud asked with a chuckle.

"I hope so—after they see a truck driven over it," Tom replied.

He made the test two days later. The whole village turned out to watch as Tom drove a heavy truck up the ramp. Bud sat with him in the cab.

"Wow! What a view!" Bud gasped, looking down over the jungle treetops.

Soon the crowd of spectators was lost to view as the vehicle rolled forward over the gleaming white span. Suddenly the truck began sliding to one side.

"The whole roadway's tilting!" Bud yelled in panic. "We'll fall off!"

"Steady, pal—the guardrail curtain will hold us up!" Tom was clutching the wheel to keep from sprawling over his seatmate.

By now the skyway had heeled over so far that Tom and Bud could see the trees almost directly below. Tom radioed for help over the truck's short-wave set before they climbed out. Arv soon arrived in a graphicopter to pluck the boys to safety.

"Whew! What an experience!" Bud gulped. His face was pale and dripping with perspiration.

"Good thing the natives didn't see it," Tom said, "or they never *would* use our skyway!"

"What went wrong?" Arv asked.

"Some of our side-beam reflectors may be out of position," Tom guessed. "Let's drop a ladder."

The young inventor scrambled down and checked the tree to which the nearest reflector had been bracketed. To his amazement, the twin-horned device was missing! The adjoining reflector on the opposite side of the skyway was also gone.

"No wonder we slid galley-west," Tom said angrily, after climbing back aboard. "Those reflectors are designed to prevent sidesway. Without them, the truck was heavy enough to put the span out of balance and heel it way over."

"More sabotage?" Bud asked grimly.

"I don't know—but I sure intend to find out!"

On hearing the news after the boys returned to camp, Creel glanced suspiciously at Luke Auber.

"I seem to recall that our great hunter was supposed to protect this outfit, Auber," he sneered. "So far, you haven't done too well."

Auber grinned coolly. "What about your so-called 'field trips' to collect specimens? Maybe you

bagged a couple of reflectors while you were at it."

Creel tried to swing at the hunter, but Tom intervened. "Cut it out, or you're through here, Creel!" he snapped. "Any other remarks you want to get off your mind, Auber?"

The hunter shrugged. "Try the Wangurus. I've noticed some of the tribesmen watching our work crews. Maybe they took a fancy to those reflectors —to use as charms or trade goods."

Tom realized that the idea was a plausible one. Taking Auber and Bud, he flew to the Wanguru village in the skywriter. The tribesmen below scampered about and gaped up at them. Tom traced several odd-looking colored designs in the air.

"Guess that ought to impress them," he said.

Bud chuckled. "The old Indian sign!"

Turning over the controls to his pal, Tom dropped a ladder and climbed down into the village clearing. Auber followed. Only Nkoru, the witch doctor, greeted them. The rest of the giant tribesmen had bowed their faces to the ground in awe.

Tom explained his mission to Nkoru.

"If any Wanguru has stolen your *grigris,* I get them back quick!" the witch doctor promised. He began to shout at the villagers harshly.

Auber translated. "He's telling them that the colored skywriting is a terrible spell you've laid on the village. They'll all suffer if the thief doesn't give back your sky-trail charms."

Presently two tribesmen stood up tremblingly and confessed. They slunk off into the bush and returned, bringing the reflectors. Nkoru tongue-lashed the cowering pair, then turned to Tom. *"Sawo!* Nkoru find your *grigris!"*

Tom thanked the witch doctor and gave him a battery-powered tape recorder and showed him how to operate it. He also promised that the colored sky symbols would fade before nightfall. Nkoru, in turn, boasted that he had frightened the villagers so thoroughly that they would never again tamper with the sky-trail *grigris.*

"Let's hope the old faker's threats work," Bud said with a chuckle as they flew back to camp.

"In case they don't, I intend to add alarm signals all along the highway," Tom decided.

Work proceeded briskly. As the skyway progressed, Tom moved his work camp forward through the jungle to keep pace with construction. He shuttled back and forth by atomicar between the main base at Imbolu and the "end of track."

A week after the Wanguru episode, Tom flew with Bud to inspect the queer dark stretch of seething, bubbling swamp at close hand. The sinister bog was only about two miles wide where the highway would cross it, but it split the jungle like a black river.

"How do we handle this hot mud?" Bud asked after they had landed.

Tom shrugged. "Plant transmitters on it, somehow. I don't think it'll be too difficult."

Tom had already radioed the *Sky Queen* to join them while the boys were en route in the atomicar. As soon as the huge ship arrived on the scene, Tom tried sinking long wooden piles, using a repelatron beam from the plane to force them downward. But the piles disappeared into the "hot mud"! Next, Tom tried to plumb the swamp with a weighted cable. To his dismay, it unreeled for hundreds of feet with no sign of bottom!

"Good grief!" Bud exclaimed. "How far down does it go—all the way through the earth?"

"Sure seems to," Tom agreed with a grin. Then he frowned. "This is serious."

It was clear that the problem called for a brand-new approach, different from anything he had had in mind. Tom dispatched the *Queen* back to Imbolu. Meanwhile, he and Bud made camp near the bog and Tom settled down to ponder the problem. How could he set foundations for his transmitters in such a bottomless morass? From the way the pilings had disappeared completely, Tom feared that even a concrete float might, in time, be sucked downward into the bog.

Next morning his thoughts were shattered by a call over the atomicar radio. "What's up, Arv?"

"Almost three miles of the skyway were wrecked last night, skipper!" Arv reported. "The natives are in a panic—they claim it was done by some kind of huge ghost animals!"

CHAPTER XVI

TERRIFYING TRACKS

THE weird news about the "huge ghost animals" sent a prickle of excitement down Tom's spine.

"Did anyone see these creatures?" he asked.

"Not as far as I can pin down the tribesmen," Arv replied, "but there's sure a lot of wild jabber going on. You'll see why when you take a look at the ground where the damage was done."

"Okay, we'll get there as soon as we can."

Soon Tom and Bud were skimming over the jungle treetops in their bubble-domed atomicar. Two miles beyond the work camp, they saw what had happened. The repelatron transmitters lay toppled and wrecked. The skyway span—no longer supported by their rays—had sagged and fractured.

On the ground, Americans and native workers were milling about, gazing at the ruins. Tom landed in a small transmitter clearing.

"Look here!" Arv said, after the young inventor had alighted. "A lot of the ground has been tramped over by the natives since last night, but I've tried to preserve some of the prints."

Tom and Bud gasped as Arv pointed out several huge, deep impressions in the soft jungle earth. The clawlike prints looked as if they might have been made by some monstrous lizard!

"Dinosaur tracks!" Bud exclaimed. "Now you *know* I wasn't seeing things, Tom!"

Other prints which Hanson showed them were rounder and broader—like outsized elephant tracks, except for projecting clawmarks.

"Brand my coyote cutlets, they're plumb spooky lookin'." Chow shuddered. "Whatever critter left them tracks, I sure never seen one in Texas!"

Apparently several animals had taken part in the weird assault on the skyway. After studying the prints, Tom turned to Auber and Creel.

"What do you fellows make of them?"

Luke Auber shrugged. "They're new to me. Only way to find out is to trail the brutes."

"I'll go with you!" Creel volunteered eagerly.

"So will I," Bud put in. "Okay, Tom?"

The young inventor caught Bud's meaningful glance. Evidently he intended to keep an eye on both.

"All right. But watch it—these babies are nothing to fool around with from the size of their prints. Better take a walkie-talkie along."

Tom would have liked to join in the hunt for the mysterious creatures, but repairing the damaged skyway was more urgent. After that, he still had to tackle the hot-mud problem.

As Auber, Creel, and Bud started off into the

bush, the young inventor plunged into the job of supervising repairs. He summoned the *Sky Queen* from Imbolu, and began cutting away the shattered span.

Meanwhile, Arv was checking the toppled transmitters. Some could be re-erected after fixing the electronic gear. Three were beyond repair.

Soon after lunchtime, Bud reported by radio. "We've trailed the monsters to a river," he told Tom. "We found plenty of fresh tracks along the bank, but we didn't see any of the beasts."

"If they're some kind of giant reptiles, they may live in the water," Tom conjectured.

"That's Creel's guess. But I doubt if the water's deep enough to hide anything that big."

Tom frowned thoughtfully. "Are they traveling together as a herd?"

"They seem to be," Bud replied. "Auber can't figure out why, since they're different species. To him, that's the most puzzling angle of all."

"I agree. And it's odd how they ganged up to wreck the skyway—unless they were battling among themselves. . . . What do you plan to do now?"

"Well, we can keep scouting along the bank," Bud said, "to see if they came out. Trouble is, we don't know whether they headed upriver or down."

Tom considered a moment. "Better give up and come on back," he decided. "Somehow I have a hunch we'll run into those animals again."

Bud chuckled dryly. "Same here, pal."

It was almost twilight when Bud and his two companions returned. The native workers, who had acted nervous and upset all day, seemed relieved that the trio had come back empty-handed.

Chow barbecued a side of beef that night. As the boys ate around the campfire, Bud remarked:

"The more I think about it, Tom, the stranger it seems. I mean, the way those dinosaurs did that midnight wrecking job and then scrammed before daylight—like a sneak raid."

"It's peculiar, all right," Tom agreed.

Bud shot a troubled glance at the young inventor. "You don't suppose that—well, that your enemy could have *arranged* it somehow?"

Tom shrugged. "It seems too fantastic to be possible, Bud. Dinosaurs are bad enough—but can you imagine anyone *bossing* a gang of dinosaurs?"

Bud chuckled. "When you put it that way, it sure does sound crazy! How's Hank making out?"

"Going great guns—no problems at all. I talked to him on the radio this afternoon."

Bud chewed thoughtfully on a piece of beef. "When that dinosaur story broke, you suspected Macklin for a while, didn't you?"

"Seemed logical, since he was the only one I had told," Tom said. "Why?"

"Well, all our troubles are happening at this end of the highway—none at the eastern end. Doesn't that clear Macklin, or any of those political troublemakers in East Ngombia?"

Tom shook his head gloomily. "They might just be trying to divert suspicion," he reasoned.

When the meal was over, Tom sat brooding in the firelight. His skyway would be of little value to the people of Ngombia if it were in constant danger of being wrecked by saboteurs or animals. Even the rank-growing jungle vegetation posed a threat, Tom realized, since it might eventually foul the transmitters.

"Bud, there's only one solution. I'll have to add a new feature to the skyway transmitters."

"Such as?"

"A special repelatron tuned to repel animals or plant life. That way, nothing can get close enough to the transmitters to wreck them."

That evening Tom air-hopped to Imbolu by atomicar. There he radioed Enterprises, using the *Queen*'s powerful transmitter, and asked for his father. Tom explained his problem and asked Tom Sr.'s help in adding the protective equipment to all future transmitters shipped from the plant.

"I'll get at it tonight, son," Mr. Swift promised. "And I'll have Uncle Ned start a production run on small units that you can add to the transmitters you've already installed."

"You're a lifesaver, Dad. Thanks."

After signing off, Tom radioed Princetown and requested soldiers to patrol the skyway day and night until the protective repelatrons could be added. An official promised immediate action.

Next day, after all the wrecked transmitters had

been repaired or replaced, Tom laid a fresh span of Durafoam over the three-mile gap in the skyway.

The following morning, after the soldier patrol had arrived, Tom took off by atomicar with Chow and Bud to return to the hot-mud bog. En route, Tom radioed the Flying Lab to join them.

"Any ideas on how to lick this mud problem?"

"Not yet. I want to analyze the stuff first." Tom frowned as he set the atomicar down neatly alongside their campsite near the bog. "My hunch is, Bud, there's some kind of intense chemical reaction going on deep under the mud, which keeps it seething—maybe even an atomic reaction."

Tom's hunch was proved correct by a radiation counter. The mud near the surface showed faint, but not dangerous, traces of radioactivity.

As soon as the *Queen* hovered into view overhead, Tom climbed aboard, taking a sample of the mud. Bud accompanied him to the ship's laboratory. Here the young inventor began making a number of chemical tests. When he heated some of the mud to incandescence and examined it with a Swift spectroscope, Tom's face became puzzled.

"What's the answer?" Bud asked.

"Its spectrum is unusual, Bud. And the frequency shift at peak intensity doesn't seem to follow Wien's displacement law."

Bud scratched his head, then grinned. "Okay. Just pretend I never asked."

"What it all boils down to is—I can't figure out

what the stuff is composed of," Tom said with a smile. "Frankly, I'm stumped."

Several hours of testing brought him no nearer the answer. Finally, Tom dispatched the Flying Lab back to Imbolu and directed the pilot to put a sample of the hot mud on the shuttle flight to Shopton that evening. Tom enclosed a note, asking his father's help in analyzing the substance.

As Chow and the boys ate supper around their campfire, Tom seemed quiet and absent-minded. He kept mulling over the hot-mud problem.

At last the three lay down for the night, with the blaze of the fire fading into glowing embers. The jungle was shrouded in eerie silence, broken only by the drone of crickets and the occasional scream of a tree hyrax.

Suddenly Tom awoke. His scalp bristled as his bedside lantern revealed a weird figure in the doorway of his tent. A tall, bony old white man stood there. His face, burned dark by the African sun, contrasted starkly with his bushy gray whiskers. The man's eyes glowed fanatically.

For a moment Tom wondered if he were dreaming. Then the old man spoke in English.

"Leave the jungle, Tom Swift!" he croaked. "I warn you, if you try to continue your highway over the bog, a terrible vengeance will strike!"

CHAPTER XVII

PILLARS OF FIRE

TOM was shocked wide awake. He threw back his blanket and started to get up from his cot.

"Who are you?" Tom asked the weird-looking old man. "And why should a terrible vengeance—"

He had no chance to finish. The stranger turned and bolted from the tent!

Tom leaped up and darted after him. The tall, bony figure was disappearing into the darkness beyond the glow from the dying campfire.

"Wait!" Tom pleaded. "You're in no danger! I only want to talk to you!"

But the intruder was already lost from view among the towering trees and dense vegetation. Tom plunged recklessly in pursuit.

The next instant he pulled up short as a huge figure suddenly blocked the way. Tom threw up his arms, but a mighty fist struck him. The young inventor toppled backward with a moan.

The next thing Tom knew, Bud and Chow were splashing water in his face near the campfire. "Whew!" Tom blinked dazedly. "What hit me?"

"We were waiting for you to tell us, pal," Bud said. "Feel okay now?"

"Y-yes . . . I guess so."

"Brand my bedroll," Chow rumbled, "we heard you hollerin' so we come runnin' out o' our tents! Then we heard a noise in the bushes an' found you spread-eagled like a dead Injun!"

"Wait a second. It's coming back to me." Tom sat up slowly and winced. He told about the old man and how he had chased him, only to be felled by some unknown giant. "A native, probably."

"You mean one of those Wangurus?" Bud asked.

Tom frowned uncertainly. "No, somehow I don't think so. His getup was different."

By now he and the others were too wide awake to go back to sleep immediately. Chow stirred up the embers of the fire and heated some cocoa. For a while the three sat listening to the chorus of insects and the soft croaking of tree frogs.

"Tom, do you suppose that old man could be the missing Professor Eldreth?" Bud asked.

"I've been wondering that myself," Tom mused. "He sure didn't speak like a college science professor—but I don't suppose anyone would after twenty years in the jungle."

"The poor hombre sounds loony," Chow put in.

"Maybe," Tom agreed. "I'd like to know what he meant by that warning, though."

"I'll bet it's not going to stop you," Bud said. "Or that whack on the head, either."

"How'd you guess?"

Bud grinned. "Foolish question, eh?"

Next morning Tom awoke full of energy. "Maybe getting kayoed last night cleared my brain," he told Bud as they ate breakfast. "I think I've figured out a solution to this hot-mud problem."

"Let's hear it, genius boy."

"Well, it's a cinch this morass is no place to erect transmitters," Tom explained. "So let's side-step the difficulty by attaching the transmitters to the underside of the skyway itself."

Both Bud and Chow stared at the young inventor.

"Brand my biscuits!" Chow growled. "You sure that clout on the head *cleared* your brain, boss? Jest how're you goin' to get the highway up in the first place with nothin' to support it?"

Tom chuckled. "I'll show you two skeptics."

As soon as breakfast was over, the group flew to Imbolu. Here Tom had five repelatron transmitters set up on the open savanna, the grassland beyond the fringes of the jungle. Next, he took off in the graphicopter and poured five separate skyway spans, each a half mile in length. The hardened surfaces were then grappled from the *Queen* and deposited on the ground.

"Now what?" Bud asked.

"I'll attach a transmitter to the underside of

each span," Tom explained. "Of course I won't be able to use the regular transmitter units. I'll have to pull the electronic gear from five of them and make some smaller housings that can be bolted to the spans."

That afternoon, while the new housings were being constructed in the main camp's machine shop, Tom was summoned to the radio aboard the Flying Lab. Mr. Swift was calling from Shopton.

"I've been working all day on that mud you sent from the jungle bog," he told Tom.

"Were you able to analyze it, Dad?"

"Yes. It's a most unusual compound, composed of several rare isotopes." Mr. Swift dictated the chemical formula, adding, "I suspect it may have important applications in aerospace technology— and also in medicine and nutrition."

"Medicine and nutrition? How so?"

"Because," Mr. Swift explained, "I discovered that traces of the same compound are present in those soil samples in your lab."

Tom gave a low whistle. "You mean the *compound* is what caused the fantastic growth of those earthworms?"

"Right, son. Doc Simpson and I are eager to experiment with it on other living organisms."

After chatting a few minutes longer, Mr. Swift said that Harlan Ames had some news for Tom.

"Remember that hood, Willie Jarvel, I told you about?" Ames began. "Well, he finally talked."

Tom felt a surge of excitement. "Then they arrested the right man?"

"They sure did. He not only admits planting the bomb in your basement, but he worked on every move your enemies made here in Shopton."

Ames reported that Jarvel had confessed to taking part in the airport kidnapping. He had been the young man in the back seat who chloroformed Kwanu's secretary. He had also driven past the Swift home in a car from which the spear had been launched.

"Jarvel says it was shot from a specially made spear gun, with a compressed-gas cartridge."

"How about that aluminum foil?" Tom asked.

"Jarvel was in on that, too—again as the driver. He says their car sped past the plant and the bundle of aluminum 'birds' was fired over the wall with some sort of homemade bazooka. But he has no idea for what purpose."

"He was just a hired hand, eh?" Tom said.

"It figures, since he's an ordinary hoodlum. Jarvel says his boss was the same man who conked you at the airport—tall fellow, bulging forehead, sharp chin, speaks with a slight foreign accent."

"That describes him," Tom agreed. "Is he the only person Jarvel worked with on these jobs?"

"Yes. He's the one who gave the orders and actually fired the spear and the aluminum foil. Jarvel knows him only by the name of Kroker."

Both the State Police and the FBI, Ames added, now had a dragnet out for Kroker.

"Okay, Harlan. I'm glad to hear all this," Tom said. "With luck, maybe they'll pick up Kroker soon—if he hasn't followed me to Africa."

As Tom emerged from the air-conditioned plane into the torrid African heat, he felt as if he were entering a steam bath.

"Whew!" Tom glanced up at the lead-colored sky. Though the sun had clouded over, the humidity seemed to be increasing. "Another reason to hurry up on this job," he thought. "A few more weeks and the rains will set in. From the looks of that sky, we may get a storm today!"

By nightfall the special repelatron housings were ready. Tom tuned the transmitters to repel the chemical compound which Mr. Swift had analyzed, then had them bolted to the skyway spans.

Next day the spans were towed through the air to the bog area. Meanwhile, native work crews had been flown in to clear a space for a regular transmitter unit on each side of the morass.

After these units had been set up, Tom poured a half-mile span on each side of the hot mud. Then began the work of raising the five prefabricated spans into position between them. Each had to be bonded with a "weld" of fresh Durafoam.

"Tom, this is really slick!" Bud stared admiringly at the first two spans. They now extended out over the bog, supported in mid-air by their own built-in transmitters. "When the whole thing's finished, it'll be a 'flying bridge'!"

"Good name for it, Bud." The young inventor

called a halt to the work for a midafternoon snack
of sandwiches and lemonade. "Let's hope we don't
run into any hitches," he added.

Suddenly Chow cocked an ear. "Brand my bees-
wax, there go them jungle drums again!"

Darcy Creel listened to the throbbing sound.
Then, with an odd glance at Tom, he translated:
"They're foretelling the doom of the young white
juju man for daring to defy the jungle gods."

Tom shrugged off the sinister prophecy.

By late in the day the "flying bridge" was completed, spanning the whole hot-mud area. Tom
and his companions were jubilant at his success.
The sky, however, had gradually grown darker
with menacing cumulus clouds.

"Looks like you finished jest in time, boss,"
Chow commented, after a glance upward.

Soon after nightfall the storm burst in full fury.
Americans and Ngombians peered from their tents
in awe. Thunder nearly deafened them as rain
poured down in sheets. Fantastic lightning discharges raced toward the hot mud.

"Wow! Regular pillars of fire!" Tom gasped.

Again the darkness was lighted by a series of
brilliant flashes. Next moment, the flying bridge
came crashing down in ruins!

CHAPTER XVIII

DINOSAUR STAMPEDE

TOM was stunned by the awesome disaster. "All that work for nothing!" he murmured. "And the repelatron gear is probably ruined!"

Bud put his hand on his pal's shoulder. "Don't take it too hard, Tom. You built it once—you can build it again."

The young inventor could only shrug gloomily. Slumping down on his cot, Tom recalled the weird old man and his strange warning. His prophecy had come true in a way Tom had never expected!

There was no way even to inspect the damage in the stormy darkness. Rain continued to lash the tents, while the jungle trees swayed and moaned in the driving gusts. Jagged lightning split the sky, followed by cannonades of thunder. Tom stretched out on his cot. "Hope the patrol's weathering this storm okay," he said. "They can go back tomorrow. We won't need them now that the protective repelatrons are installed."

The storm gradually abated, and by daybreak, when the boys awoke and went outside, the sky was clear. But a fresh shock was in store for them. The wrecked bridge had fractured completely under the fury of the storm and had now sunk without a trace into the hot mud!

"Jumpin' jets!" Bud exclaimed. "That's what I call weird!"

Even the Americans gaped in awe, while the natives stood in huddled groups near the edge of the bog, muttering fearfully. *"Sho-sho-go binu oba asara na je!"* one of them said to Tom.

Darcy Creel translated. "He's saying that Sho-sho-go has devoured the bridge in his awful anger. Remember, Sho-sho-go is the god of thunder and lightning. He seems to be the special god of this swamp."

Tom's eyes lighted with sudden interest. "Thanks for the information, Darcy." The man's remark had just given Tom a fresh slant on the night's disaster. "Tell the men I'll talk to them later. In the meantime, they have nothing to fear."

As the boys walked toward the campfire, where Chow was preparing breakfast, Bud asked a bit sheepishly, "Tom, you don't suppose there's anything in this jungle voodoo stuff?"

"Definitely not. Why?"

Bud shrugged. "Well, the way your bridge was destroyed—it's gone completely. I'm not superstitious but, man, I've never seen anything like those lightning bolts last night!"

Tom stopped and faced his friend. "Look, fly-boy, I'll admit the lightning was unusual. I'd like to know more about those terrific discharges myself. As for what happened to the bridge, that was strictly a natural phenomenon. The lightning knocked out the repelatron transmitters, leaving the bridge with no support. So it collapsed, fractured, and sank into the bog."

"What about that old man's prophecy?" Bud argued.

"Creel just gave us the answer to that."

Bud looked puzzled. "I don't read you, pal."

"Don't you see? If this hot-mud swamp is sacred to Sho-sho-go, it must be because terrific thunder and lightning storms often occur over this area. So the old man was just banking on the law of averages that we'd run into trouble."

"*Hmm.* I see what you mean." Bud's eyes narrowed. "But *why* are thunderstorms frequent here? Don't tell me Sho-sho-go sends them whenever he gets angry!"

Tom chuckled. "Far from it. The storms simply tend to concentrate here due to the thermal updrafts from the hot mud. In the rainy season, I'll bet thunderheads repeatedly form over the bog."

"Okay, genius boy, what about those pillars of fire last night?"

"There you have me," Tom admitted. "We

know that lightning depends on a separation of positive and negative ions inside the thundercloud. But why they should build up to such terrific potentials is another question. Want a guess?"

Bud grinned. "That'll be good enough for me."

"Well, it may be that the faint radiation from the hot mud causes ionization in the surrounding air. This then forms a high-conductance path for the discharge. But remember, that's *just* a guess."

"Sounds great. So what do we do now?"

"Rebuild the bridge, naturally."

After breakfast, Tom called the native workmen together. They were still fearful and upset by the night's disaster. Some were even clamoring to return to their village. With Creel translating, sentence by sentence, the young inventor made a short speech.

"When I built the bridge," Tom began, "I did not realize Sho-sho-go was so powerful. So I did not use my strongest juju. The bridge was wrecked. But Sho-sho-go has not dared to harm *me!* Now I will build the bridge again. This time I will plant some very strong *grigris* in the hot mud. I promise you these *grigris* will swallow up any more thunderbolts that Sho-sho-go may send!"

Tom ended by saying that extra rations would be given out that day, so his Ngombian friends could enjoy a great feast while he was working to prepare his *grigris*.

The news was greeted with loud cheers, clapping, and stamping. From the looks on the natives' faces, Tom's speech appeared to have changed their minds.

"Brand my elephant stew, you handled 'em jest right, boss!" Chow chuckled. "Like I always say, the way to any hombre's heart is through his stomach—African *or* American!"

"Let's hope your *grigris* turn out to be just as successful," Creel put in dryly. "If they don't, it may take more than food to get these men back on the job."

Tom said nothing, but Bud snorted angrily, "Stop being such a dill pickle, Creel!"

Bud and Tom flew back to Imbolu. There he set to work at once in his Flying Lab, designing the devices to "swallow thunderbolts." Bud watched as the young inventor sketched out a strange-looking design at his drawing board.

"What in the name of science is it?" Bud asked.

Tom chuckled. "Just an ordinary lightning rod. But it's supposed to be a high-powered magic gizmo, remember? So it has to look the part."

Instead of being a straight vertical rod, Tom's device zigzagged and spiraled crazily. It also had odd treelike branches. From the bottom a cable would extend down into the mud.

Tom explained that the device would be attached to the bridge spans by rigid brackets made of his vacuum-celled Durabuoy, which was actually lighter than air. The brackets would be insulated with Tomasite. A number of lightning rods would be spaced along both sides of his flying bridge.

"That offbeat design should wow 'em," Bud prophesied. "It even had me doing a double take!"

By putting every available man to work in the base machine shop, Tom had the queer devices ready that same day. Next morning he began the job of reconstructing his flying bridge. New spans had to be poured and special transmitters prepared to support them. But, with the speed of practice, the work proceeded rapidly.

By the following afternoon the bridge once again soared gracefully over the bog. Then the fantastic-looking lightning rods were flown in from Imbolu and bracketed in place. The weird shapes of the *grigris,* sprouting on each side of the bridge, made the natives' eyes pop.

"Wo! Idán aràbàra!" they murmured in awe. "Tom Swift make very strong magic!"

Meanwhile, construction of the eastern and western halves of the skyway had been leaping ahead, day by day. Tom estimated that a few more days of work would see the two parts joined to the bridge.

Full of enthusiasm, Tom flew with Bud over the whole route in the *Sky Queen.* On the way back he hovered above Hank Sterling's work camp while the chief engineer climbed aboard.

"How does she look, skipper?" Hank asked.

"Great, Hank—in fact, terrific!" Tom answered. "I think I'll radio Princetown and offer Kwanu and his staff a preview of the skyway."

The official was delighted at Tom's invitation.

"Tom Swift make strong magic!" they murmured

When the Flying Lab arrived at the Princetown airport next morning, several Ngombian dignitaries were on hand for the flight. They gasped with excitement as the skyway came into view, arching above the jungle treetops. Tom listened with a pleased smile to their glowing comments.

"Incredible!" Kwanu declared. "My dear Tom Swift, your engineering genius is even beyond what we had heard!"

When they landed back at Princetown, he asked the young inventor how soon the skyway would be complete. After Tom had named a date, Kwanu said, "The country will declare a national celebration on the day the skyway is ready for use!"

Tom returned to Imbolu, then air-hopped by atomicar to his camp at the western "end of track." Another half-mile span had already been added in the short time since Kwanu's inspection tour.

"Won't be long now, pal!" Bud told him.

Tom nodded proudly and glanced at the sky, which was clouding over. "Maybe those fancy lightning rods will get a tryout sooner than I expected," he remarked. "Let's hope things won't be held up tomorrow if it does rain."

The young inventor pushed construction harder than ever that afternoon in case of a possible delay. By nightfall, after a hearty meal of Chow's broiled steak and roast potatoes, Tom was only too glad to tumble onto his cot. Within moments he was deep in slumber.

He was aroused hours later by wild cries of

fear. Tom leaped from his cot, still groggy with sleep, and rushed from his tent. What he saw jolted him like an electric shock.

Monsters of nightmarish size were surging forward out of the darkness, plunging among the tents and scattering the sleepers!

Tom glimpsed a huge lizardlike creature that might have been a tyrannosaurus, scuttling on two legs. Other behemoths, resembling brontosauruses or brachiosauruses, with long, swaying necks and serpentlike heads, were crowding close behind.

"Good night!" Tom gasped. "A dinosaur stampede!"

The camp was in panic.

"Run for it!" Auber shouted again and again.

Men were fleeing in every direction—anywhere to escape the trampling titans. Tom turned as he felt his arm clutched from behind. It was Bud.

"Don't just stand there, pal!" Bud shouted above the din. "Let's get out of here!"

There was no time to argue. The boys plunged into the bush. The next moment they felt themselves seized in a grip of steel. A giant figure had materialized out of the darkness!

Tom sensed that it was the same native who had knocked him unconscious on the night of the old white man's visit!

CHAPTER XIX

THE MONSTER MAKER

TOM and Bud struggled frantically against their assailant, but the giant stunned them by banging their heads together. He bound the boys' arms to their bodies, using a single long rope.

Suddenly the man gave a blood-chilling yell, which jarred Tom back to semiconsciousness. What followed was so unbelievable that Tom felt as if he were dreaming. Several dinosaurs came smashing through the undergrowth!

The huge native slung the boys like saddlebags across the back of one of the smaller beasts. Then he clambered nimbly up the ridged tail and spine of a lizardlike monster that reared on two legs. Straddling its back, the giant grabbed a rope tied around its neck. With another yell he thumped the creature with fist and heels, and the animals started off.

The beasts lumbered along at a speed surprising for their size. Other dinosaurs joined them as they passed the wrecked camp, and the herd headed northward into the darkness.

To Tom and Bud the journey was like a nightmare. They were buffeted by every movement of the ponderous animal, and slashed by jungle growth.

Presently Tom realized they must be fording a river as water splashed high on every side. Then the beasts emerged onto dry land again, and the trek continued. To add to the eerie atmosphere, a gale began to blow, heralding another storm.

At last the weird procession arrived at a stockade enclosure. The giant dismounted, untied the two boys, and propelled them roughly into the stockade. Then he herded his beasts inside and barred the gate.

Tom guessed that the enclosure must cover several acres. Just ahead stood several outbuildings and a lighted bungalow. A bearded man came out and strode toward the boys.

Tom gasped. This was the same old man who had uttered the warning about vengeance.

"Professor Eldreth?" Tom asked coolly.

The elderly man stopped short and regarded Tom with piercing eyes. "You know me?"

"I've heard of you!" Tom snapped. "And I'd like an explanation of why you caused our camp to be wrecked and had us kidnapped!"

Tom's words stung Eldreth. "You have brought disaster on yourself!" the professor ranted. "I warned you not to continue. But you paid no heed. For years I have pursued my experiments peacefully. Your highway would have brought people to the forest and ruined my lifework!"

"The highway will serve the people of Ngombia," Tom replied. "Besides, it runs *above* the jungle and wouldn't interfere with your work." Tom added, "Incidentally, I'd like to hear about your experiments. My father and I have studied your technical papers. We're interested in your theories about the breeding of throwbacks."

Professor Eldreth's angry expression relaxed as he realized that Tom was sincere. "I've often heard of Mr. Swift," he said. "You too, I'm told, are an outstanding scientist. Very well—perhaps you can appreciate what I've done."

He led the boys inside his bungalow. The giant native followed, keeping a watchful eye on the two prisoners. Tom glanced around the room at the array of scientific equipment. It was a fully equipped biological laboratory!

"Most scientists sneer at my work," Eldreth confided. "But here, working alone in the jungle, I have proved my theories! I have succeeded in breeding throwbacks to the dinosaurs that lived millions of years ago!"

"It's amazing!" Tom said. "How did you do it?"

"The race of dinosaurs died out, as you know, leaving no descendants," Eldreth replied. "But the crocodilians evolved from the same stem. I therefore began my experiments with crocodiles taken from these jungle rivers."

"You mean you turned ordinary crocodiles into those monsters out there?" Bud put in.

"In a way, yes. I took crocodile eggs and treated them with X rays and chemicals to cause mutations, or changes. This produced freak animals— some with characteristics of earlier reptiles far back on the scale of evolution."

Tom nodded. "Then you bred the freaks."

"Exactly," Professor Eldreth said. "In this way, I was able to telescope the evolutionary process in a *backward* direction. Finally I produced a creature much like the thecodonts—the ancestor of both crocodiles and dinosaurs."

Eldreth led the boys outside and blew a whistle. Tom and Bud gaped as several creatures scampered in response. They were like large lizards, about the size of police dogs, but running erect on powerfully developed hind legs.

"Good grief!" Bud gasped. "How'd you like *them* as watchdogs, Tom?"

"No thanks," Tom muttered.

Meanwhile, Eldreth had gone back into the bungalow. In a moment he emerged, carrying some pieces of raw meat, which he threw to the thecodonts. They seized the food with their clawed forelegs and gobbled greedily.

"From these you developed your dinosaurs?" Tom asked.

"Yes. I concentrated on developing animals with a bone structure like the saurischians—the reptile-hipped dinosaurs. I succeeded in producing not only two-legged meat eaters like the tyrannosaurus, but also the heavier four-legged plant eaters like the brontosaurus and brachiosaurus." Professor Eldreth got a lantern and said, "Come along. I'll show you."

He led the boys off through the compound. Tom and Bud watched furtively for chances to escape, but the giant native followed close behind them. Presently they came in view of a group of huge dinosaurs, resting quietly among the trees. The beasts blinked in the light as Professor Eldreth raised the lantern proudly.

"There are the results of my years of work!"

"I still don't see how you managed to get your results so quickly," Tom said. "Even twenty years seems too short a time to retrace so much of the evolutionary process."

Eldreth's face took on a sarcastic smile. "My scientific colleagues jeered when I reported finding a growth hormone in a jungle bog."

"My father has analyzed that compound," Tom said. "It just causes giantism."

"By itself, yes," Eldreth replied. "But with other chemicals added, it also *speeds up* growth to a startling degree. By injecting the formula into an egg embryo, one of these creatures can be raised to full size in two months!"

Tom gasped. The news of Professor Eldreth's work would hit the scientific world like a bombshell—if he and Bud returned to tell the story. What *was* behind tonight's raid? Had Eldreth masterminded all the moves to block the skyway project?

"I'm sure I'll learn more if I can gain the professor's confidence," Tom thought.

As they walked back toward the bungalow, he remarked, "The theropod dinosaurs, like the tyrannosaurus, were supposed to be quite fierce. How have you managed to control them?"

"When raised by humans and treated kindly, they are easily managed," Eldreth replied.

Suddenly the old man stopped and glared at Tom. "That is another reason why your highway must never be built! What would happen to these dumb, helpless beasts if the jungle is opened to civilization and ignorant fools stream in?"

Tom said, "A game preserve could be set aside for your animals. No hunters—"

"Do you think I believe that?" Eldreth shouted. "For years I was hounded and ridiculed. Only Mbonga helped me carry on my work. Tom Swift, no one is going to destroy the results of our efforts!"

The old man's eyes glowed fanatically. Mbonga, the giant, seemed to realize the professor was becoming irrational.

"Master, please not talk more!" he begged. "Come back to—"

Mbonga's words were cut short by a crack of lightning. The bolt struck a tree nearby, splitting it wide open. The four watchers were dazed by the compression wave from the lightning.

Before they could recover, the shattered tree came crashing down, the upper end striking

Mbonga and pinning him underneath! Professor Eldreth gave a cry of grief and rushed to his servant.

"Now's our chance! Let's go!" Bud tugged Tom's arm and ran toward the stockade wall.

"No, Bud! Wait!" Tom called. "We can't go and leave the poor fellow like this!"

Bud ran back. "You're right."

The youths hoisted the tree sufficiently for Eldreth to drag Mbonga free. They carried him into the bungalow and laid him on a cot.

The servant's scalp was gashed, but apparently he had suffered no broken bones. Tom assisted in treating the cut and sponging Mbonga's forehead. Presently his eyes opened.

As the giant native saw Tom and Bud standing unguarded, within easy range of the doorway, he sprang up and grabbed them.

"No, Mbonga!" Professor Eldreth said, and told of the rescue. The black giant's eyes opened wide in surprise. Then he dropped down on one knee and touched first Tom's, then Bud's hand to his forehead.

"You Mbonga's friends . . . Mbonga thank you."

"I, too, thank you," Professor Eldreth said in a choked voice. "Mbonga has been my faithful helper. Without him I'd be lost."

"There's no need to thank us," Tom said. "But maybe now you'll explain about tonight's raid on our camp and why we were captured."

The old man sighed heavily and sat down on a chair. "I guess I was mistaken in opposing your highway. And I regret having assisted your enemies—especially after the way you refused a chance of escape, in order to save Mbonga." Eldreth paused, then went on, "Several white men came here days ago and asked me to help wreck your highway. I agreed for the sake of my experiments."

"Who were the men?" Tom asked.

"I do not know. The leader is tall, with a large forehead and pointed chin."

"Kroker!" Bud exclaimed.

Tom nodded. "The same man who conked me at the airport and hired Jarvel to assist him."

Eldreth said that he had agreed to let Mbonga take the dinosaurs and smash down some of Tom's transmitters. But he had refused to expose his valuable animals on any more such raids, fearing that Tom might take measures to trap or destroy them.

Later Eldreth had been persuaded to let his animals be stampeded through Tom's camp and to have Mbonga seize the boys. The stampede was to scatter Tom's work crew so raiders could sabotage the highway transmitters.

"The men plan to tamper with the transmitters in such a way that your highway will collapse as soon as it is put into use," the professor explained. "They hope the road will then be condemned and the Swifts' reputation ruined."

"Of all the low-down tricks!" Bud exploded.

"Wait a minute! They can't sabotage the transmitters!" Tom said. "The protective plant-and-animal repelatrons will prevent them from getting close enough to do anything."

Professor Eldreth quickly dashed Tom's hopes. "I was told that someone in your own group will provide the raiders with a remote-control device which you use to turn the repelatrons on or off for maintenance work."

"Must be Auber or Creel!" Bud cried out.

Tom paced back and forth. "If only I could communicate with the *Sky Queen!*" he exclaimed.

"I have a two-way radio set," Eldreth said. "The men who came here brought one so they could contact me at any time."

The boys were jubilant. Tom quickly radioed the *Queen* at Imbolu and ordered a Swift pilot, Slim Davis, to take off in the skywriting graphicopter. "The raiders probably will be using lights," Tom said. "If you see them, point out the spot with an arrow in the sky."

"Now what?" Bud asked, after Tom signed off.

The young inventor grinned. "Ever hear of tanks on the hoof?"

"Wow! I get it—a dinosaur blitzkrieg!"

Professor Eldreth agreed to lend Tom several of his dinosaurs, provided that he and his servant accompany the boys. Tom and Bud found it hard to mount the beasts, but Mbonga showed them how. They took off, driving a small herd of the

The dinosaur riders crashed through the jungle

faster-moving animals. A frantic ride through the darkness followed.

Suddenly Bud pointed to the sky and cried, "Look! Slim has spotted them!"

A luminous arrow was taking shape over the forest. Guided by it, the dinosaur riders crashed through the jungle. As they approached the skyway, a glow of light became visible through the trees. Men with lanterns and guns were at work in one of the transmitter clearings! The saboteurs gaped as the beasts and their riders burst into view.

"It's Tom Swift!" one cried out. "Get him!"

A hail of bullets greeted the riders!

CHAPTER XX

JUNGLE JUGGERNAUTS

TOM and his companions ducked behind their mounts, and the wildly aimed bullets took little effect. Tough-hided, and with only simple nervous systems, the beasts were almost impossible to bring down.

Seconds after the first volley of shots, the dinosaurs were bearing down on the saboteurs. The huge creatures were frightened and enraged by the loud, stinging gunfire. They reared and plunged, spreading panic with their trampling hoofs and fearsome jaws. The enemy raiders fled in terror, tossing away their guns.

"Don't let them escape!" Tom shouted, jumping from his mount. Bud and Mbonga followed.

The three dashed after the fleeing saboteurs. Tom caught up to a thickset man, the leader. He grabbed the man's shoulder and yanked him around. Hans Macklin!

"So you're the sneak who's been behind all our

troubles!" Tom swung a furious roundhouse punch at his enemy's jaw.

Macklin staggered and fought back, snarling like a leopard at bay. Bud, meanwhile, had gone for Kroker, whose oddly wedge-shaped face had made him recognizable. The husky flier with a single blow sent Kroker reeling backward.

Mbonga had already seized two of the raiders and banged their heads together. Then he streaked in pursuit of a third victim. The giant overtook his quarry easily and dragged the fleeing man back. Tom had downed Macklin.

"Nice going, genius boy!" Bud grinned as he counted the five prisoners. "Looks as though only one got away."

"Mbonga trail him when daylight come," the native promised.

Bud covered the captured saboteurs with one of their own discarded rifles. Tom collected the other guns. Meantime, Professor Eldreth was making soothing noises as he calmed and rounded up his herd of dinosaurs.

By the light of the saboteurs' lanterns, Tom inspected the transmitter. Presently he removed a small transistorized assembly. "Pretty neat," he announced. "This is a remote-control device of their own which would have enabled them to shut off the main repelatron sweep beam after the skyway was open."

"You'll have to check all the other transmitters,

too," Bud said. "And we still don't know who slipped them *your* remote-control gadget."

Tom's eyes had a steely glint as he said, "Maybe Mr. Macklin can tell us."

Macklin glared back at him in silence. Kroker was sullenly nursing his injured jaw. The other saboteurs squirmed nervously but said nothing.

"Hey! Someone's coming!" Bud exclaimed.

In a moment figures appeared among the trees beyond the transmitter clearing. The lantern light revealed their faces—they were Tom's own men! Luke Auber was in the lead.

"I assume those monsters are under control?" Auber called out.

The newcomers stared in awe at the dinosaurs, which were now resting quietly or browsing among the leafy vegetation.

"Don't worry—they won't bite." Tom waved the men forward.

One of them was Darcy Creel. His hands were tied!

"We ran into this bloke a little ways from here," Auber said. He explained that after rounding up some of Tom's work crew, he had sighted the arrow in the sky and had come to investigate. His party had heard the gunfire and soon afterward sighted Creel. "He was in complete panic and babbled out a confession about helping Macklin," Auber went on. "We found this on him."

Auber held out a small electronic device. Tom

recognized it at once as his remote-control switch for the protective repelatrons.

"So Creel was the double crosser," Bud said. "I guess I owe you an apology, Auber."

The tall hunter grinned. "For that matter, I owe you chaps an apology. I'm a private investigator. Kwanu will vouch for me—I took on this job by arrangement with the Ngombian government."

Tom and Bud stared at him in amazement.

"In that case, maybe you can tell us what Macklin's game was," Tom said.

Auber nodded. "Once your highway is built, it will mean closer government supervision of his mining setup. Macklin has had a free hand till now. He has been treating his native labor ruthlessly and cheating the company for his own gain. Once the two provinces were linked, he would be exposed. He *had* to block your project."

"How did you find out all that?" Bud asked.

"It was my job," Auber replied. "Afro-Metals, Limited, began investigating Macklin soon after Ngombia became independent. The company officials were afraid he might give them a bad name among the new African nations, so we disclosed our suspicions to the Ngombian government and asked permission for an agent to accompany your group to guard against any moves Macklin might make against your project. And now you chaps have caught him dead to rights."

Tom gestured toward Kroker. "Know anything about this man?"

"Yes," said Auber. "He's a strong-arm thug whom Macklin hired to keep his native workers in line. Kroker's a skilled electronics man, too."

"That explains who masterminded tonight's plot to kill our transmitters," Tom said coldly.

Kroker turned pale. "I didn't mastermind the plot!" he whined. "Macklin did. Swift, he tried to kill you with that poison-gas idol!"

"Shut up, you fool!" Macklin roared.

"The game's up," Kroker retorted.

"You're the one who sent the idol!"

"And you arranged the whole deal—poison gas and all!" Kroker shouted. "I was only following orders!"

Tom chuckled inwardly at the way his ruse of accusing Kroker had worked. Kroker continued to talk freely. Macklin had sent him to the United States to scare Tom and keep him away from Africa. Kroker had sent the devil doll and released the fake news story about Enterprises winning the highway contract. This was done to force Tom to admit or deny that he had taken on the project. Through government friends in Princetown, Macklin had learned that the Swifts were to be asked by Kwanu to undertake the job, and had arranged the theft of the Burlow plans from the Princetown files.

Kroker also admitted he had hired Willie Jarvel

to help him with the airport kidnapping, the spear incident, and the launching of the aluminum "birds" to flutter down over Enterprises.

"I take it you also recruited Darcy Creel to assist in the plot?" Tom put in.

Kroker nodded. He said the purpose of scattering the aluminum foil was to give Creel a chance to rummage through Tom's papers and uncover whatever plans he had made.

Kroker added, "Creel showed us his invitation to the masquerade. We forged one for Jarvel."

Creel, reddening guiltily, blurted out, "I didn't know they'd try to plant a bomb. When I found out, I warned your security chief, Tom!"

Shamefaced, Creel insisted that the only reason he had agreed to help Macklin was that he was badly in need of funds. "I'd lost a lot of money on a recent business scheme," he added.

The journalist said he had been offered high pay if he could join Tom's expedition and keep Macklin's men informed about the work. He had sneaked out of camp to talk to them the first night after the project got underway. It was his cigarette Auber had found.

"He tipped us off about the chance to wreck the transmitters!" Kroker snapped.

While the raiders were operating in the jungle, Kroker's men had learned about Professor Eldreth from natives and enlisted his help.

"You're a pack of fools!" Macklin exploded bitterly. "I knew I couldn't trust you! That's why

I had to come along tonight—to make sure the job got done. You've bungled the whole business, and now we'll all wind up behind bars!"

"Where you belong," Auber remarked. "I'd say that about finishes the case—eh, Tom?"

The young inventor nodded and glanced apprehensively at the sky. "From the sound of that thunder, we'd better get back to camp."

After warm handshakes, Professor Eldreth and Mbonga departed with their dinosaurs. Tom and his men took the prisoners to camp, where Chow and Arv were busy restoring order. Both were overjoyed to see Tom and Bud.

"We learned over the radio from Slim that you had things pretty well in hand," Arv said.

The storm broke moments later. Everyone scurried to get under canvas. Throughout the night and the following morning, rain pelted down from a sky lighted by shafts of lightning.

Not until late afternoon was Tom able to inspect his flying bridge. He was jubilant to find it undamaged.

"Your *grigris* did the trick," Bud said with a grin. "You great juju man, Tom Swift!"

Auber, meanwhile, had taken the prisoners to Princetown. He told Tom that Creel, an American citizen, probably would be sent to the United States to face charges. Kroker, too, might be extradited by the American authorities. Macklin and the rest would stand trial in Ngombia.

By the following week the repelatron skyway

was complete. A national celebration was declared on the day that Tom Swift's great engineering achievement was thrown open to the public.

The Ngombian prime minister cut a ribbon at the western ramp, and a gaudy procession of native potentates and officials drove over the skyway. Loud bands and dancers in tribal costume accompanied the triumphal parade.

But Tom's greatest satisfaction came when he saw the ordinary people of Ngombia begin using the long jungle span that now united their country.

Later, at Government House, Prime Minister Luongo pinned Ngombia's foremost decoration on Tom. "Your amazing repelatron skyway has joined our two provinces into one nation," he said. "Thanks to you, Tom Swift, we can now develop our resources and build a better life for our people."

Then the prime minister turned to Professor Eldreth, who was standing by in a new white suit with his proud and grinning assistant, Mbonga.

"As part of Tom Swift's reward—and at his suggestion," Prime Minister Luongo told the professor, "we are setting aside a section of our national forest as a permanent park and game reserve for your dinosaurs. We plan to build a laboratory in which you can carry on your experiments."

Professor Eldreth thanked the prime minister and gripped Tom's hand warmly. "As a scientist yourself," he murmured, "you know how much this means to me. Due to your efforts, I have already received messages from all over the world, acclaiming my work."

The young inventor grinned. "I hope you'll feel the same way when the world starts flocking to your door, Professor. The Eldreth Dinosaur Park probably will become Ngombia's greatest tourist attraction."

That evening, after a state banquet, Tom and Bud boarded the *Sky Queen* and took off for home.

"Brand my baked beans, it'll sure feel good to hit the ole U.S.A. again!" Chow said.

"Right," Bud agreed. "Oh, to sleep on a real mattress, away from that steamy jungle! What are you looking forward to, Tom?"

"Well, let's see—it's about time for another undersea cruise, isn't it?" Tom smiled as if he were already planning his *Aquatomic Tracker*. "After seeing all those dinosaurs, I might even go hunting for a real live sea serpent!"

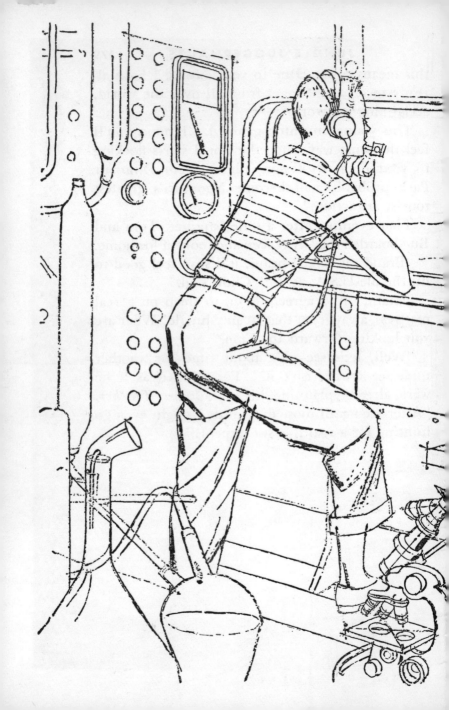